# THE PRINCE AND HIS BEDEVILED BODYGUARD

## PARANORMAL PRINCES BOOK 1

### CHARLIE COCHET

**The Prince and His Bedeviled Bodyguard**

# ACKNOWLEDGMENTS

A big thank you to my alpha reader Macy Blake for all her support and encouragement. To all the amazing readers who've been so supportive, standing by me through all these ups and downs, thank you.

Thank you to my wonderful editor Desi Chapman who knows my writing so well, and to my beta reader Amy DiMartino for her honest and invaluable feedback.

Thank you to Leslie Copeland who is always there to help and her amazing team who've done so much for me. Thank you to all the incredible people who continue to pick up my books and show them love. You're truly an inspiration.

# SYNOPSIS

## Prince Owin

Being a fierce predator—not at all adorable, despite my graceful stature—the last thing I needed was a bodyguard. Especially a wolf shifter, whose presence alone was an insult to my princely principles. As Prince of the Ocelot Shifters, I prided myself on my infallible feline instincts, uncompromisable dignity, and flawless fashion sense. If having a canine follow me around at all times wasn't bad enough, I now faced the most important moment of my entire life. The time had come to prove I was worthy of my crown. If only I could find a way to get rid of the pesky bodyguard.

## Grimmwolf

When the King of All Shifters asked me to guard Prince Owin, I admit I had no idea what to expect. Cat shifters tend to be a little intense, not to mention kinda cranky. Owin was no exception, though he seemed crankier than most. Being his bodyguard was proving to be one of the greatest challenges of my life—but not nearly as great as convincing him there was something special between us. When Owin is faced with a perilous quest to prove his worth, I was determined to keep him safe, even if the same couldn't be said of my heart.

# PROLOGUE

## KING ALARICK

TODAY WAS THE DAY. How very exciting!

"The princesses did exceptionally well. I'm so proud of them." I sat back against the pillows Jean had fluffed for me as he did every morning. He puttered around my royal chambers, opening the many curtains in preparation for a new day. Bright sunlight cascaded through the windows, casting a warm glow throughout the expansive ivory room and reflecting off the many gold accents. What a gorgeous morning. Perfect for a quest.

"They're certainly worthy of their titles, Your Majesty. I'm sure the princes will be no different." Jean finished his task before bringing me my breakfast tray. The scent of freshly brewed coffee and bacon crisped to perfection wafted through the air, and my stomach grumbled. One would think I hadn't been fed in decades. He placed the tray over my lap, and I smiled affectionately at the small vase with the single flower. Jean had been bringing me my breakfast since I could remember—which was quite a long time for an immortal—and he always remembered the flower.

"What?" Jean asked, a bemused smile on his handsome face. "You're quiet."

"Nothing. You're so very good to me," I said, beaming up at him. He might not be able to see me smile, but he could sense it. He'd been at my side for so long, he didn't need his heightened senses to see me or even know what I was thinking. Jean had lost his sight a lifetime ago, but he'd found other ways to "see." He chuckled and shook his head at me as he made his way over to the ivory couch to the right of the room.

"Well, someone has to keep you out of trouble," Jean teased.

I laughed and took a sip of my coffee as he sat. Today his suit was a plum color that looked particularly good with his fair skin. Whereas my dark hair always seemed in disarray, his was combed and neatly parted to one side. He sat where he did every morning, one long elegant leg crossed over the other. As I ate my breakfast, he went over my itinerary. When all the boring stuff was out of the way, we came to the fun part.

"On to the princes, then." I rubbed my hands together in glee. "Who's up first?" Done with my tray, I moved it to one side and got out of bed. Jean was immediately at my side, helping me with my robe.

"Prince Owin of the Ocelots."

"Ah, yes. He's adorable, isn't he?" I crossed the room to my walk-in closet. *What to wear?*

Jean stepped up beside me and ran his fingers over the shoulders of the suits in front of me, each one tailored to fit my frame and stature, no two alike in color, fabric, or style.

"Wear the red three-piece suit with the gold embroidery and the black robe. I wouldn't let him hear you say that, Your Majesty, but yes, he is adorable."

"And feisty. This is going to be fun." I pulled the suit off the rack. "Good choice."

"You're a little bit evil, my king."

I snapped my jaws at him, making him laugh. "Come now, Jean. He needs it. We both know it. Some of my children are rather...."

"Royal pains," he replied with a knowing smile.

"Well put, Jean."

"Thank you, My Liege"

I handed the suit to Jean, who then busied himself laying it out on my bed while I went about my morning routine. Once I'd brushed my teeth and showered, I returned to Jean.

"Are you sure this is a good idea?" Jean asked from behind me.

"One second. I forgot to grab underwear." I turned, not realizing he stood so close, and ran into him. "Goddess above. I'm so sorry, Jean." I grabbed him to steady him, and he put his hands on my waist.

"You're naked," he said through a gasp.

I chuckled. "I'm always naked before I get dressed."

His cheeks turned a lovely shade of pink, which was a first, and I put my hand to his brow. He jumped with a start.

"Goodness, are you all right?"

"Yes. Sorry, I, um, must be a little off this morning. Those pesky fairies were playing outside my window again last night."

"I'll speak with their queen. They've been warned

about playing tricks on the staff. Our agreement was they could enjoy the palace grounds and gardens, provided they behave themselves." I couldn't help but worry. Jean wasn't merely my advisor; he was my truest friend. I felt lucky to have him at my side. "Are you sure you're all right?"

Jean smiled brightly. "Absolutely. As I was saying, do you think this is a good idea?"

Taking Jean's word that he was fine, I fetched a pair of red boxer-briefs and pulled them on before returning to the bed. "Of course it's a good idea. My ideas are always brilliant."

He cocked his head to one side and scrunched up his nose. "Are they?"

I arched an eyebrow at him. "You don't think so?"

"Remember your disco phase in the seventies? You had a disco ball installed in each room, and every morning when the staff opened the curtains, they were blinded. Poor Alistair tripped over a footrest and fell off the balcony. Good thing the rosebush broke his fall."

I cringed. "Poor Alastair. Margaret was pulling thorns out of his butt for hours." I waved a hand in dismissal. "Perhaps not my brightest idea, but *this* idea is brilliant. Every generation of shifter nobility brings with it a new set of challenges. The more my shifter children are exposed to humanity, the more I question whether the decision to bring our worlds together was a wise one."

I quickly pulled on my socks, then slipped into the shirt Jean held out to me, followed by my pants and then the vest. Once everything was buttoned, Jean held my jacket out to me, and I slipped my arms into the sleeves. "Many believe I made a grave error in exposing my children to humans, but the world has changed so much, Jean. Magical creatures across the globe are dying, fading into nothingness. Their stories lost and forgotten. I won't allow that to happen to my children. I won't. Humans are keeping us all alive, even if they don't realize it."

Our magical world was as complicated as the human one. A melting pot of legendary creatures and monsters. Unlike the human world, we magical beings found ways to coexist. It was either that or perish, and we were all quite fond of living, especially with our survival becoming more challenging with every millennium.

As King of All Shifters, my kingdom stretched across the globe, each shifter species ruled by its own shifter prince or princess. Every magical creature species possessed a monarchy of sorts, a family to rule over them, keep the peace, and look out for them.

Some creatures preferred to live in secret, hidden away in forests, caves, or bodies of water, while others preferred to live among humans. Some even formed their own humanlike towns and cities, hiding in plain sight. Very clever, my children. But then the apple doesn't fall far from the tree, does it? Humans had no idea. I found it amusing they never thought to question why there were so many lumberjacks in Longview, Washington. Beaver shifters. A whole city of them, one of many actually. Who did the humans think invented lumberjacking? Jean's hand on my shoulder snapped me out of my thoughts. I had a habit of letting them run away with me.

"You did what any good father would have done. You've taught your children to survive. If that means walking among humans, then so be it. We must all adapt to this changing world or be left behind." Jean smoothed down the front of my jacket, then buttoned it up for me. He placed a hand on my shoulder, a little lower than usual so it covered part of my heart. His smile warmed me. I laid my hand over his.

"Thank you, Jean. What would I do without you?"

"You would be sad."

His words were unexpected and squeezed my heart in a way no words ever had. "Yes, I think I would be." We stood in silence for a slip of time, our hands touching. "You know, it's not necessary for you to wear that bandage around your eyes." He was so self-conscious about anyone seeing his eyes. To me they were beautiful—pools of fathomless aquamarine. Jean feared the lack of pupil would frighten those around him, but I couldn't imagine anyone being afraid of such a wonderful creature. As close as we were, Jean had never entrusted me with what manner of magical creature he was, and his scent was unlike anything I had ever come across. It hurt a little, but I trusted him with my life. He had his reasons.

"I know." He placed his hand to my cheek, his thumb caressing my skin. "We should go. Mustn't keep the brat waiting."

I threw my head back and laughed. "Oh, how I do love you, Jean." Throwing my arm around his shoulders, we headed for the door.

Jean's reply was so soft, I barely heard him. "I love you too, Your Majesty."

"This is going to be such fun."

# CHAPTER ONE

## PRINCE OWIN

THE TIME HAD COME.

I had finally been summoned by King Alarick. Next to my coronation day, this should have been the most exciting moment of my life, but was I jubilant over the occasion? No, I was vexed, oh so very vexed. Why? Because I was forced to share this moment with the most infuriating creature in all existence!

Grimmwolf.

Goddess above, who named this guy? Grimm was the most annoying wolf I had ever come across. Did I mention he was infuriating? First of all, he was a wolf. He *smelled* like a wolf. *Ugh, so gross.* It wasn't bad enough King Alarick assigned me a new bodyguard—one I couldn't get rid of—but a wolf? Of all the magical creatures in all the realms, why a canine shifter? The very idea had me instinctively drawing my claws out and hissing as I stomped up and down the ornate carpet in front of the king's throne room. I, Prince Owin of the Ocelot Shifters, regal and pretty, was saddled with an overgrown, hairy *dog*. This was wrong on so many levels.

I tried to distract myself with my surroundings. It wasn't every day one was called to *the* palace. As the King of All Shifters, King Alarick's palace was like its own city, nestled among lush forests on Heart Island in the St. Lawrence River. *My* palace would fit in his palace. His was grand in design, reminding me of several of the human palaces—all ivory walls and gleaming marble floors, gold accents, and red carpets—with the exception of the decor. Where most human palaces featured the royal family's human ancestors, the many paintings and statues around King Alarick's palace featured our shifter history, proudly displaying all manner of shifters, from the most delicate and beautiful to the most terrifying.

No one knew who birthed King Alarick, but we did know the sun was involved, hence the golden suns featured throughout the palace's decor. It was really quite breathtaking. Spinning on my heels, I smacked into a wall and bounced off. Oh, wait, not a wall. Stupid wolf. Why did they all need to be so darn tall? Not that I envied his stature. Not. At. All. Naturally wolf shifters were bigger than ocelot shifters, and bodyguard wolves were even bigger than regular wolves, so it wasn't the brute's fault he took up so much space. I glared at the beast.

"I can't believe you chose *that* to wear to see the king," I hissed, waving my arms at his general person. "Humans invented fashion for a reason. Look at me." I stood tall and motioned to my tailored blue suit and cute little bow tie, which I could totally pull off because I was fabulous. "Now look at you."

Grimm shrugged. "This is my uniform. It's what I always wear. Everything in my wardrobe is exactly the same."

"Exactly!"

"That makes no sense. You make no sense."

I poked him in the chest. "I don't have to make sense. I'm the prince."

"You're something all right," Grimm muttered.

"What did you say?" I narrowed my eyes at him, sizing him up once again in case by some miracle the guy had shrunk. Over the last six months that I'd been stuck with him, I'm not proud to admit I'd been tempted to smack him on more than one occasion, but that would have required having a chair brought to me, and that sort of indignity was beneath me. I could have shifted and bitten him, but again, not how the Prince of the Ocelot Shifters should comport himself. Or so I'd been told by my advisor. Several times. Whatever. I was the prince! If I couldn't randomly bite someone who annoyed me, what good was my title? I was a cat, for crying out loud. Might as well tell the birds they shouldn't chirp or fly.

Grimm pointed to the large painting on the wall beside us. "Isn't that an interesting piece of art?"

"Don't try to distract me, you—" I made the mistake of glancing to where he pointed. "Oh, it is, isn't it? Look, there's a little rabbit in its burrow!" I loved rabbits. Granted, I mostly enjoyed eating them, but they were fluffy and cute when they weren't being eaten. They were an ocelot favorite, but then so were most small creatures that we could hunt and catch. Not that I couldn't catch something bigger than myself if I wanted, but that's what the royal hunters were for. As if I'd get my fur dirty.

"You're right," Grimm replied, sounding amused.

"Of course I am. I'm—"

"The prince," he said with a smile. "Don't worry, I haven't forgotten."

"I loathe you."

"And *I* think you're adorable."

I hissed at him. *Adorable?* I was a predator! I was fierce! Fierce, I say! Stature wasn't everything you know. Grimm was clearly compensating for something with his size and height.

"You're only strengthening my case, really."

"And *you* look like you're about to go to war."

He seemed to consider this. "As I've been assigned by the king to guard you, that's a fair observation. And a fact."

I chose to ignore that. "What's with the gray camouflage?" Honestly, of all the clothing options available to us. The wolf had no sense of style whatsoever. My image had suffered greatly since his arrival. At least *I* thought so.

Grimm pointed to his face—"It matches my eyes."—then his head. "And my hair."

"I'm sorry, are you telling me you wear an all gray military uniform because it matches your eyes and your hair?" He couldn't be serious, could he? Then again, he was a canine, and they were... easily distracted. Perhaps I should have done some research on wolves when he'd been assigned to me?

"I'm a gray wolf. See what I did there? Actually, I just like gray. But hey"—he pointed to his chest—"this part's black." He wiggled his fingers, drawing my attention to the black fingerless gloves. "See? Also black."

"And what's with all the pockets?" I motioned to his pants. "Who needs *that* many pockets?" No response. *Ugh*, whatever. "You're a bodyguard. Shouldn't you be wearing a suit or something?"

"That's a little cliché, don't you think?"

I rolled my eyes and started pacing again. This day was nerve-racking as it was, without adding *him* into the mix. "I don't understand why King Alarick would assign you to me. I really don't."

"Probably because you ran off every other bodyguard you ever had, and anyone who hasn't been your bodyguard refuses to be in the same realm as you?"

I rolled my eyes. "Such drama queens."

"Or," Grimm said, holding up a finger. "Hear me out now. Or, maybe you being a complete and utter jerk is the reason they wouldn't piss on you if you were on fire. No offense."

My jaw nearly hit the pristine red carpet. "*What?*"

"I said—"

"I heard what you said! That's the problem. Aren't bodyguards supposed to be *silent?* Shouldn't you be standing stoically, brooding while you practice your menacing scowl?"

"Do I look like a cat to you? I'm a wolf. We don't brood." He paused in thought. "Okay, maybe some of us do, but generally we're quite cheerful by nature. Unless you try to take our food. That would be bad. I enjoy conversing, smiling, and wagging my tail. Did you know a lot of humans don't realize wolves can wag their tails?"

I stared at him. "Oh my Goddess, my bodyguard is an idiot."

"That's harsh."

"Why are you *smiling?*" Who was this guy? All he did was follow me around and smile *for no apparent reason.*

"Why not?"

I was going to explode into sparkly prince confetti at any moment, I just knew it. He was going to make me burst.

An earsplitting clatter made me jump and I spun around, claws at the ready. A member of the King's staff was on the floor, picking up pieces of scattered silverware. I hurried over and dropped to my knees.

"Here, let me help you," I told the young girl. Her scent revealed her to be a fawn shifter. Her big brown eyes widened, and her cheeks flushed.

"Oh! It's not necessary, My Prince."

"Nonsense." I waved a hand at her in dismissal. As if it were a hardship. "What's your name?"

"Ayla."

"Well, Ayla, did you know that the kitchen is one of my favorite places? Next to the library and gardens, of course," I rambled on in the hopes she might feel more at ease since she was all but shaking from nervousness. "So much so that Faline—my head chef—has to chase me out more often than not. But can you blame me? It's always so warm in there, and it smells so good." I picked up the tray that was bigger than her and stood. Turning to Grimm, I handed it to him. "Hold this." I swiftly helped her gather all the fallen silverware and placed it on the tray. "Where would you like this delivered? I'll have Grimm carry it for you."

Ayla smiled sweetly. "Thank you, My Prince. I can take it from here. I'd simply tripped earlier. Head in the clouds."

"Are you sure?" She was a tiny little thing. I was certain the tray weighed more than she did.

She nodded and curtsied before taking the tray from Grimm. "Thank you again, My Prince." With a big smile she walked off, singing a little tune to herself.

I turned to Grimm and arched an eyebrow at him. "You heard her. I'm the prince."

"Doesn't make you any less adorable."

I hissed, ready to give him a princely thrashing when

the huge gilded doors opened, and the king's advisor, Lord Jean Eldrich, appeared. "The king will see you now."

Grimm smiled wide. "The king will see us now."

"I heard him!"

With a frustrated growl, I marched into the throne room, ignoring Grimm walking beside me, his long strides making it so he was always at my side no matter how much I quickened my pace.

The throne room was impressive with all its ivory and gold, the only color coming from the vibrant red and gold throne, but then the king who sat upon it was far more impressive. King Alarick was bigger than Grimm, broad shoulders, muscular, strong, with pitch-black hair and amber eyes you could see the cosmos in if you stood close enough. They were a little freaky, to be honest. Not that I would tell *him* that.

My power came from my people, allowing me to control their shift. Technically, I could control Grimm's shift, but a prince had to have a really, *really* good reason to force a shift in another species. Any prince or princess who abused their power would be stripped of it along with their title. They'd be banished from their realm. King Alarick was immortal and drew his power from all the shifter nobility, allowing him to change into any shifter he reigned over. I wondered how a prince could get in on that action. Being immortal, I mean, not *action* as in sexy times with the king, because *ew*. He was a father figure to us all, and that was not my kink. Not that I had any. Or maybe I did and didn't know it? Being a prince sort of limited my dating options, and wow, maybe now was not the time to think about this.

"Welcome, Prince Owin of the Ocelot Shifters, and welcome Grimmwolf of the Grimm Wolves pack."

I turned to Grimm. "You're named after your pack?" *So lame.*

Grimm blinked at me. "Um, no. My pack is named after *me.*"

Why would a wolf pack name themselves after a bodyguard? I turned a questioning look to the king.

"Wolf shifter hierarchy is a little more complicated than your feline shifter hierarchy due to packs. Each pack has its own alpha, but like all my shifter children, they are all still ruled by one prince or princess. Grimmwolf comes from a long line of nobility," King Alarick offered with a proud smile. "The Grimm Wolves pack is the monarchy wolf pack. Grimm's mother is the current alpha of the pack, while Grimm's father is the Prince of All Wolf Shifters. Grimm is an alpha wolf and the prince's successor."

"*What?*" I glared at Grimm. "You're an alpha and the next wolf shifter prince and you didn't tell me?" No wonder he was so damned smug and mouthy. Wait. I spun back to face the king. "Why is the prince's heir my bodyguard?" I wasn't fond of the twinkle in the king's eye.

"I needed someone who could keep up with you, and Prince Grimmshaw saw this as the perfect opportunity for his son to learn about interspecies relations. Appointing him as your bodyguard seemed like a win for both of us."

Interspecies relations? Unbelievable! Not like I had a choice. I narrowed my eyes at Grimm. "This changes nothing."

Grimm shrugged; his ridiculous smile plastered on his face. "Sure."

The king cleared his throat. "Let's get started, shall we? As you know, Prince Owin, when a new generation of prince is crowned, he must prove he is worthy to rule. Each prince must complete a quest. Should the prince fail in his quest, he will forfeit his crown, his title, and his powers. He will be unworthy of his people. Your quest is to retrieve a priceless artifact from the Cù Sìth."

Easy-peasy. "Wonderful. How long do I have to get my entourage together?"

The king arched a thick black eyebrow at me. "Honey, you're not Beyoncé. You don't get an entourage."

"Pardon?"

"You get Grimmwolf."

"Pardon?"

"Are you an ocelot or a parrot? Owin, your bodyguard is going with you. He is all you get to take on your quest. Which starts the moment you leave this room, by the way."

I was horrified. No, beyond horrified. "I'm not sure I understand. I need to prepare. I need food, bedding, and the appropriate Jimmy Choo's. I—"

"No need to worry." The king motioned for Lord Eldrich. "Jean, the magic satchel, please."

Oh good. I was being given a magic satchel. I sighed with relief. At least until Lord Eldrich appeared with a brown leather bag that was somewhat on the large side and a little rustic-looking for my taste. Did it come in different styles? The king moved his gaze to Grimm.

"Grimm, I gift you this satchel. Anything you desire is at hand. You have but to think it and retrieve it from the bag."

Wait, *what*? "You're giving the satchel to *him*?" What was happening right now?

The king nodded. "Should you need something, merely ask your bodyguard."

Ask? I squinted at him, confused. What did he mean by... ask? Wait, I was supposed to ask *him* when I needed something? That was absurd! I didn't ask for things. I was—

"The prince. I know," Grimm said with a chuckle.

I gasped. "Can you read my mind? Are you one of those creepy seer wolves?"

"Nope." He leaned in and tapped my forehead. "I've just gotten pretty good at reading your scowls."

I smacked his hand away. "How dare you touch me!"

Grimm reached into his magical purse—satchel my cute little ocelot tail—and handed me something. "Here."

"A chocolate bar? I don't need a chocolate bar! And certainly not from *you*." I glared at him for good measure. How dare he! How dare the king! How dare everybody! Ugh, this was a nightmare. I should have stayed in bed, watching humans do stupid things on YouTube.

Grimm waved the chocolate bar at me. "But it has little crunchy bits in it. Your favorite."

That was true, and it only pissed me off more. "You are so infuriating!" I spun on my heels and stormed toward the door.

"Good luck on your quest," the king called out after me. "You'll do great. I'm sure of it. Watch out for squirrels. They're thieving little bastards!"

"Your Majesty, it was one squirrel. You really need to stop your war on squirrels."

"But do I, Jean? Do I?"

Heavy sigh. "Yes, you do. We're talking about a cinnamon bun."

"A delicious cinnamon bun that I will never get to enjoy!"

"Come. Let's go to the kitchen. We'll have Chef make you something equally delicious."

"Fine. But if a squirrel tries to get into the kitchen, I expect you to annihilate it."

"I'll be sure to vanquish the evil beast, Your Majesty."

"Good. I'm in the mood for cookies."

I was surrounded by weirdos. Grimm appeared beside me, and I cursed his long legs. He waved the chocolate bar at me again. "Are you sure you don't want it?"

Stopping abruptly once I reached the hall, I spun toward him. "Wave that in my face one more time and I'm going to bite you. Manners be damned."

"Aw, that's not nice. You shouldn't go around biting handsome wolves who offer to put tasty things in your mouth."

My eyes almost popped out of my skull, and my face felt like it was attempting to set itself on fire.

Grimm cocked his head to one side. "Wait, that sounded wrong."

"You think?" His smile was about to get knocked off his face.

"Oh, you're blushing!"

"I am not." The very nerve! I snatched the chocolate bar out of his hand. "Now will you leave me alone?"

"You are blushing. Your cheeks are all pink—"

"In anger! I'm blushing in anger! Now shut up. The quicker we get this over with, the better." Surely once I finished my quest and proved my worth to the king, he'd see I didn't need this ridiculous wolf at my side. Straightening my bow tie, I nodded to him. "Well, hop to it."

"Ookay. Well, King Alarick said the treasure we need is with the Cù Sìth."

"Perfect. Who are they, and how do we find them?" If we hurried, we might be home in time for dinner. Today was Taco Tuesday, and I'd be miffed if I missed it.

"You don't know?"

I rolled my eyes at him. "Why would I need to know? They're not my people and therefore not my problem."

"But, they're part of our world."

"And I'm just supposed to know every magical creature in the world?" Wasn't that what the internet was for? Or staff. I had an entire council of people to worry about that sort of thing for me.

Grimm looked confused. "Yes. Part of being a leader is knowing who your allies and enemies are."

I really did not enjoy being schooled by a wolf. "Grimm?"

"Yes?"

"I don't care." I wiggled my fingers at him. "Reach into your little purse—"

"Satchel."

"Reach into your little purse and do whatever it is you have to do to get us to the Cù Sìth."

"How am I supposed to do that?" he asked, motioning to the bag now slung across his wide chest. I could have sworn the bag was bigger when Lord Eldrich had been holding it out. Had it shrunk?

"I don't know how. Reach into your magic purse—"

"Satchel."

"Reach into your magic purse and ask it to take us."

"Right. I'll simply pull out a magical portal that will take us where we want to go."

"Sarcasm is very unflattering on you," I said, folding my arms over my chest as he shoved a hand into his bag and pulled out what looked like a glowing blue orb.

"What the—" Grimm dropped the orb, and we both jumped back. To my utter disbelief, it spread upward and sideways until it was roughly the size of a large doorway, a forest appearing inside. "Hmm. What do you know? A portal that will take us where we want to go."

How cross would the king be with me if I accidentally

pushed Grimm off a cliff? Or left him with the Cù Sìth? Not like he didn't have plenty of wolf shifters. What was one less in the grand scheme of things?

Grimm narrowed his eyes at me. "You're not leaving me behind."

How did he do that? "Are you sure you're not a seer wolf?"

Grimm didn't look impressed. "You're right. I'm a seer. My curse is that I'm limited to visions of you being a jerk."

I opened my mouth to respond, then thought better of it. "Can we just go?"

"As you wish, Your Highness." He bowed and motioned for me to go ahead. Clearly, he thought I was an idiot.

"What if it's a trap and I step through and burst into flames? You go first."

"Your generosity knows no bounds, my liege. Fine. I'll go first, but if I meet my demise, my blood is on your hands."

I shrugged. "I'll get over it."

"So mean." He shook his head at me and stepped through. On the other side, he turned and held his arms out. "See? All good. Wait...." He gasped and clutched at his chest. "What's happening to me? It burns!"

"Grimm?" My heart lurched in my chest, and I stepped up to the portal.

"I can't," he gasped, falling to his knees. "I can't...."

"Can't what!" Oh my Goddess, oh my Goddess. I never expected him to actually burst into flames! I flailed around feeling utterly helpless. "What do I do? Is it flames? Are you bursting into flames?" I frantically looked around. "I don't see a fire extinguisher!" Not that I knew how to use one. I'd just have to toss it at him and hope he could do it himself.

"I can't...." He gasped for breath. "I can't... believe you fell for that," he said with a laugh.

"I'm going to kill you!" I darted into the portal, ignoring his laughter as he took off, his long legs putting him out of my reach in a heartbeat. "I hate you!"

"Admit it! You were worried about me," he called out from across the field.

"Worried you'd die and I wouldn't be able to pry the magic purse off your cold, dead, dog-smelling corpse!"

"It's a satchel!"

# CHAPTER TWO

## GRIMM

I SHOULD HAVE TOLD HIM. Maybe. Probably.

Who was I kidding? The moment Owin said he didn't know about the Cù Sìth, I might have rejoiced a little in his impending misery. I wasn't sure what Owin despised most —that he couldn't get rid of me or that I was a wolf. Not that it mattered, because the king was making it up to me. King Alarick was known for being quite mischievous, and at times sneaky. Part of his charm. As I stood behind Owin and waited for one of the Cù Sìth to arrive, I could barely contain my glee. I was awful, terrible. I should have been ashamed of myself, but I wasn't. If I'd been in my wolf form, my tail would have been wagging out of pure joy.

A summer wind rustled the leaves of the trees around us and flowed through the tall grass of the rolling hills. We faced a sea of green towering mountains and above us a blanket of brilliant blue. Somewhere in the distance, a river of sparkling water trickled by. A breeze ruffled my hair, and I inhaled the heavenly scent of freshly dewed grass. The Scottish Highlands were beautiful, and so very peaceful. Shame that peace was about to be shattered.

I took a step to the side so I could see Owin's face better. He peered at me, wary, but I remained silent. This was going to be good. So good. I needed to commit every moment to memory so I could call upon it later.

"Who enters the realm of the Cù Sìth?"

Owin's eyes opened so wide I thought he might hurt himself.

"You have got to be kidding me," he spat, his hands balled into fists at his sides.

I was quite proud of myself. I didn't laugh in his face like I wanted to. The range of emotions that crossed his features was everything. Okay, *range* was too strong a word. Two emotions crossed his face: stunned disbelief and anger, and oh boy, was he angry. Why? Because the magical creature he'd been sent to retrieve his artifact from, was a dog. A giant green fae hound, to be precise.

"This is your fault," he hissed at me.

"My fault? How is this my fault?"

"I don't know. I just know it is."

The Cù Sìth was about the size of a bull, with shaggy green fur and a braided tail. His eyes glowed red, and he smelled of wet grass. And dog. Wet dog. It was glorious.

"Whatever." The prince stood before the Cù Sìth hound, nose turned up and shoulders rounded back. "I am Prince Owin of the Ocelot Shifters. I demand you hand over my prize."

I cringed. Demanding things of magical beasts, especially spectral hounds, was never a good idea. The Cù Sìth cocked his large head to one side as he studied Owin. I had no idea how this was going to go. The Cù Sìth might give us what we came for, or he might decide to carry us off to the fae underworld.

"I do not have what you seek, young prince," the Cù Sìth said with a thick Scottish burr.

"I'm sorry, what?"

Oh, this was so much worse than getting carried off to the fae underworld. *One ticket to the underworld, please!*

"The item you seek is not here."

"Excuse me a moment." Owin spun on his heels and stomped off toward the forest. I thought it best to stay where I was, especially after his shriek scared birds and fairies out of the trees. The rant that followed was pretty epic. Wow, so many curses. Where did he learn *that* word? I turned back to the Cù Sìth and smiled.

"So, uh, how's the whole harbinger-of-death thing going?"

"It's good. I mean, it's definitely more of a challenge these days. Hunting humans was a lot easier when they were traveling on foot or by carriage. Do you know how hard it is to get a human to hear your deadly howls when they're blasting Taylor Swift in the car?"

"Yeah, that's tough. Still making off with nursing women?"

"Oh no. We're gender neutral now, so we make off with everyone and let the fae decide what to do with them."

I nodded. "Still terrifying. But good for you. Equality is important."

"Thanks, mate. I appreciate that."

"I, um, better go check on His Highness. I'll be right back."

"Sure."

I headed to the trees Owin had disappeared behind,

gingerly stepping around them and biting down on my bottom lip at the sight of Owin throwing a hissy fit. Literally. He'd shifted to his ocelot form and was now hissing and swiping his claws at whatever he came across. He was so darn cute. All thirty pounds of him. Turning, he spotted me, and he did that super creepy-ass thing cats do where they arch their backs and tails really high, then walk sideways on their hind legs. It made me shiver. Cats were *so* weird.

"Hey," I cooed, crouching down. "How are you doing, big guy? Throwing a little tantrum, are we?"

He meowed, then hissed at me, and I reached into the satchel. "Oh, look! A tiny roast chicken. Is this you being hangry right now?" Clearly that was the wrong thing to say, because he launched himself at me. I jumped to my feet, and he latched on to my boot, all four paws wrapped around my leg as he bit me.

"You know, I'm feeling a little attacked right now. I'm just trying to help, so maybe bring the hostility down a notch? Also, these are Kevlar and leather, so I can't feel your tiny ocelot teeth through them. How about you have a snack, shift back into your human form, and we talk about this?"

He tried biting me a few more times, but realizing he wasn't getting anywhere, he shoved himself off me and snatched the chicken out of my hand. He trotted away with it, carrying it up a tree. I had a feeling this was going to be a long, *long* quest. Taking a seat on the grass, I waited as he ate his tiny chicken. He ate very loudly for something so small.

When Owin was done, he scampered back down the tree and shifted. I reached into one of my pockets and pulled out a silver canteen, which I extended to him. His wariness made me smile.

"What is that? What are you giving me?"

"It's water. You need to stay hydrated."

He narrowed his eyes at me before marching over and taking it from me. Several long gulps later, he handed it back.

"Better?"

"*You're* better," he hissed.

"That makes no sense. Why are you so angry?"

"Because this quest should have been over by now! I should have arrived, been given whatever stupid magical treasure I was supposed to get, return to the palace, get blessed by the king, and go home so I could continue the more important quest of getting rid of *you*. Instead, I'm not home plotting how to get rid of you. I'm stuck here. With you."

"So, what you're saying is, you're angry because you're spoiled *and* an ass. Gotcha." Good thing he was a shifter. A nonmagical human's blood pressure would have been through the roof.

"I should throw you in the dungeon!"

"You don't have a dungeon."

"Then I'll have one built and *then* throw you in it!"

"Maybe you can get one from the humans? They flat-pack everything. Even houses. There's this place called Ikea—"

"Shut up!"

"Fine." I was just trying to help. I motioned behind us. "We should probably not keep the Cù Sìth waiting."

He made a noise I couldn't decipher. A combination of annoyed and disgusted. Spinning on his heels, he marched off. I was at his side in two strides, taking in his stylish blond hair and bright amber eyes. He was pretty for sure, with fair skin, pink pouting lips, and a petite, sinewy body. His tailored suit accentuated every curve of his body, and his ass was especially nice to look at. Unfortunately he was a spoiled royal pain in *my* ass, though he did have moments where I could see behind the grumpy kitty, but whenever he noticed I was watching him, the walls came up in full force.

Owin stopped several feet from the Cù Sìth. "If you don't have my treasure, who does?"

Again with the demands.

The Cù Sìth smiled. "Hellhound."

Oh, we were so screwed.

"Are you kidding me?" Owin fumed. "Another *dog*?"

I turned to the Cù Sìth. "What he means to say is, thank you for your help. Good luck with your, um, hunting and kidnapping of humans for the fae underworld."

"Thanks. Good luck with, uh"—the Cù Sìth nodded toward Owin—"that."

Owin's eyes went wide, and his face burned bright. "*Excuse me?*"

Not wanting to get dragged to the underworld, though I was starting to question whether perhaps I was already there, I quickly reached into my satchel—because damn it, it was a *satchel* and not a purse—and thank the Goddess, pulled out a glowing blue orb denoting a portal. I tossed it onto the grass, grabbed Owin by the arm, and launched him through it, his yelp very satisfying.

"How dare you!" Owin fumed. "No one manhandles me!"

"Maybe they should," I said, stepping through.

His gasp was very dramatic, but that was Owin in a nutshell. He opened his mouth to no doubt let me have it with both barrels but instead raked his gaze over me, his cheeks turning a bright pink before his eyes landed on my mouth. His eyes slightly widened, and I would have given my magic satchel to know what he was thinking.

"What?" I asked, my voice lowering as I stepped closer. He sucked in a sharp breath and took a quick step back.

"What are you doing?" he all but squeaked.

"Nothing. Talking. We're just talking," I replied, taking another step closer to him, knowing his next step back would be his last, since his path was about to be blocked by a tree.

"Well, talk over there," he demanded, though I noticed there wasn't much conviction behind his words. He stepped away as predicted, another gasp escaping him when his back came up against the tree. I took advantage, placing one hand to the side of his head and smiling down at him, our bodies only inches apart. Even if nothing came of it—and I *knew* nothing would come of it—I couldn't help wanting to see if my hunch was right.

"Owin?"

"Prince Owin," he corrected with a haughty lift of his chin. "Or Your Highness. Either of those would be...."

I hummed as I bent at the waist to nuzzle his temple. His hair was soft, and he smelled of flowers. And cat. The cat part didn't bother me as much as I'm certain my canine scent bothered him. He smelled good. Really good. The quiet whimper he let out hit me harder than expected.

As close as I stood to him, I was careful not to scent mark him. As an alpha, scent marking was serious business. Even more so if nobility was involved. That would practically be a marriage proposal, and considering he would gladly push me off a cliff if the chance presented itself, probably not a good idea to mark him as mine.

"Owin?"

"Prince Owin," he insisted, his voice breaking. Clearing his throat, he lifted his gaze, his face so close I felt his hot breath on my skin. "Oh, you're, um, you're far too close."

"Am I?"

He nodded. "Yes. Your, um, eyes are more silver than gray."

"Are they?"

"Why do you keep answering my questions with a question? You're so annoying."

Despite his words, they weren't accompanied by anger or frustration. I smiled, my stomach tightening at the way he sucked in a sharp breath.

"We, um, we should go," he said, inching slowly away from me before turning and briskly walking away.

Interesting.

I followed him out of the forest and stopped when he did. "Is this a parking lot?" he asked, looking around.

This was so much worse than I thought.

"Is that a... bar? That's a bar, isn't it? Where humans go to drink that god-awful beverage. What do they call it? It's yellow and smells like pee."

"Beer?"

"Yes, that's it. I've been dying for a good mai tai." He tapped a finger to his lips. "Though I wonder if this place even serves cocktails." He sniffed the air. "Smells like sweat, humans, and... dog. Ugh, I can't get rid of the beasts!"

"No offense taken," I said before grabbing him by the shoulders and turning him to face me. "Okay, you need to stop and listen to me."

He rolled his eyes. "When do I ever listen to you?"

"Point taken, but this time, you need to actually listen to me. The hellhounds aren't dogs. The name says it all. Hell.

Hound. Hounds of hell. You can't go in there making demands or insulting these guys. Their alpha is the alpha of alphas. He's really scary."

"Pft. Your wolf form is huge."

"His hellhound form is bigger. And they have flames in their eyes. *Flames*! Did I mention the hell part?"

"It'll be fine. I'm a prince. I'll demand—"

"I just said no demands!"

He looked affronted, genuinely affronted. Like I'd shifted into my wolf form and taken a dump in his shoes. Not that I've ever done that before. Certainly not to my ex-boyfriend who cheated on me with a two-headed snake. Snakes don't even have lips! I mean, come on. Okay, not one of my prouder moments. Anyway, I needed Owin to listen. Getting dragged to the fae underworld by the Cù Sìth was bad. Getting dragged to hell by a hellhound? So much worse.

"I'm sorry. What part of hounds of hell did you not understand? Was it the hounds part or the hell part? It is their job to literally drag your ass to hell. And I'm not talking about just humans. I'm talking about magical creatures. How do you not know any of this? You're a shifter prince. Your people live among humans. If anyone found out about them—"

"Yes, I know. I know what hellhounds do. Everyone knows what they do." He waved his arms. "Ooh, big scary hellhounds. Yes, yes, we've all heard the stories."

I wanted to strangle him with his own pretentious little bow tie.

"Can I help you?"

I turned and managed to suppress a sigh of relief that we hadn't been met by the hellhound alpha of alphas.

"Hi, I'm Grimm," I said, extending my hand to him.

He nodded in greeting and shook it. "Solomon."

My smile faltered. Not the hellhound alpha of alpha, but *the* alpha hellhound, which was terrifying. Why the king sent us here, I had no clue. Before I could open my mouth to say anything else, Owin spoke up.

"I am Prince Owin of the Ocelot Shifters."

"Good for you."

"I demand you hand over what is mine."

Solomon narrowed his eyes. "Demand, huh?"

"Yes."

We were doomed.

# CHAPTER THREE

## PRINCE OWIN

"It's very simple, really, much like you." I ignored Grimm's gasp. These canines were so damned sensitive, and not very bright, if you asked me.

The hellhound narrowed his eyes and took a step forward. "What did you call me?"

I wasn't about to be intimidated. "Look, why don't you scamper off and fetch me my prize like a good boy." I put my hands on my knees and smiled at him. "Who's a good boy? *You're* a good boy. At least you will be once you fetch me what I ask for. Go on. Fetch." Isn't that what canines did? They loved to fetch. A hellhound should be no different, right?

"Oh dear Goddess," Grimm said with a whimper.

I turned my attention to him and rolled my eyes. "Honestly, I don't see what all the fuss is about."

Grimm shrieked—a most unbodyguard-like sound—and

I followed his horror-stricken face to the source of said horror.

"Oh my Goddess!" It was huge. Like, *massively* huge. "His eyes are on fire! How—what—why are his eyes on fire? Oh Goddess. Hellhound!" I screamed and took off, barreling past Grimm into the forest as fast as I could. "Eat *him*, eat *him*!" I was too precious and far too pretty to be carted off to hell by a black beast!

"You're a little shit, you know that?" Grimm shouted, leaves dispersing through the air as he sped past me.

"Get back here, you long-legged bastard!" I shifted into my ocelot form, screeching a meow at the sight of the black hell beast tearing after me. Some bodyguard I had! If I got dragged off to hell, he was *so* fired! I darted through the pitch-black woods, running as fast as my paws allowed, hopping over logs and fallen trees. The dark wasn't a problem for me. Of course, that also meant it wasn't a problem for the hellhound. Could hellhounds climb trees? Maybe if I climbed a tree...? A shadow loomed over me, and I yowled. They were far more terrifying up close.

I was about the size of its tail and feared he'd step on me, squishing me like a bug. A glowing blue light up ahead caught my attention, and just as the hellhound opened its jaws, something swooped me up. It took me a moment to realize Grimm had me by the scruff. *Ew*, I was in the jaws of a wolf! I tucked my legs under me and prayed he wouldn't drop me. I hadn't been carried like this since I was a kitten. It was quite embarrassing. Stupid wolves and their stupid ideas! We'd made it through the portal when everything went to hell. Thankfully, not literally. I managed to catch sight of the hellhound sitting on his side of the portal as I soared through the air. Grimm had tripped on something, yelped, we both went flying, and now gravity was doing its thing.

I twisted my furry little body and put my legs out, landing on my feet. And that's why being a cat was awesome. No way had Grimm landed on his feet. Another yelp resonated through the woods, and I cringed. That didn't sound good. Shaking myself from nose to tail, I remained in my ocelot form in case we needed to take off running again. The portal had closed with the hellhound on the other side, which was great. Rain poured down, which was not. Trotting toward the smell of wet dog, I flicked my tail in princely fashion and rounded a large tree, a small meow of surprise escaping me.

Grimm lay at the base of the tree not moving. I noticed the skid trail through the mud and flattened grass and realized he must have tripped and gone sliding into the tree. I bounded over, then paused when I got close. His fur was covered in mud from his muzzle to the tip of his tail. I meowed, but he didn't move. Gingerly, I approached. Thank the Goddess he was breathing. Another meow and I was met with a low whine. Was he hurt? Had he... hurt himself saving me? Why would he do such a thing?

Carefully, I inched closer, sniffing at his muzzle. His pink wolf tongue poked out and licked me. With a hiss, I lashed out on instinct, swiping my claws at his muzzle, making him yelp and jump onto his paws. He sneezed, and I hissed at him again. He was fine? How dare he worry me like that! I hissed and meowed at him with all my furry fury, but all he did was sit there and stare at me. Did he think this was funny? How was I supposed to finish my quest now? This was all his fault! I hissed and lowered myself to the ground ready to pounce on him, but he stood and shook himself off, slinging mud at me and covering me from head to toe. I yowled and bounced, throwing myself on the grass and rolling around in an attempt to get the mud off my beautifully spotted fur.

That's what I got for worrying about the cretan! I didn't need anyone, least of all *him*. Stinking of dog-scented mud, I gave up. It was over. How was I supposed to go back to the king empty-handed? I flopped onto my side, defeated, no longer caring about my stinking fur or the puddle trying to drown me where I lay. I shivered at the cold but remained where I was, not bothering to move when Grimm stood over me and whined. At least the rain was washing away the mud. That was something. Too bad it couldn't wash away the stench of failure.

Grim nudged me with his muzzle, and I couldn't even be bothered to swipe my claws at him. I closed my eyes, then let out a startled meow when I found myself lifted off my paws. What the— Where was he taking me? How dare he! *Leave me alone to wallow in self-pity, you hairy fiend!* How dare he crash my pity party! I had no choice but to hang there as he carried me off like some helpless kitten. This was so degrading. Did my title mean nothing to him? Ears flattened, I bided my time. He'd have to put me down eventually, and then I would strike with all the fury of an ocelot prince. He was in for it now. In so much trouble. All the fury.

We approached what appeared to be a large mound covered in ivy and moss. Oh, it was some kind of cave or den. Wait, he expected me to take shelter in a *cave*? I would rather freeze to death. As he entered the cave, I hissed and the brute dropped me—opened his jaws without warning and dropped me. He was lucky I landed on my paws. Giving myself a good shake, I sat and took in the space around me, which was just about big enough for the both of us, and nothing but dirt and rock.

Grimm didn't seem to be concerned in the slightest, and I stared, stunned, as he simply curled up and laid his head on his paws. Oh my Goddess, was he going to sleep? That's it? Just like that, he was out. What about *me*? I had no bed, no pillow, no blanket. Ugh, it was cold! I shivered from my wet fur. The least the brute could have done was build us a fire. Some of us didn't have frizzed, puffy fur to keep us warm. Was it my fault my fur was sleek and smooth? My paws were cold. I hated when my paws got cold. I shook several raindrops off one and let out a soft mew.

Maybe I shouldn't have clawed at him. He *had* saved my life at the risk of his own. I guessed. If he'd been awake, he could have pulled some blankets out of his purse. I loved being a shifter. I loved magic. I didn't have to worry about undressing or where my clothes went when I shifted. Because magic. Now that I thought about it, that was *the* question shifters were asked most often by other magical creatures. No one was impressed by the fact I could turn into a cute little ocelot, no. They wanted to know where my underwear went. How should I know? The universe swallowed it up and then gave it back. That sounded kinda gross and weird. "Magic" sounded much more glamorous.

*Look at him.* Sleeping like we hadn't been chased by a hellhound, or like I hadn't failed my quest. Oh Goddess, I was the first prince in the history of princes to fail his quest! Okay, maybe I wasn't. I had no idea, to be honest, but it felt that way. I refused to admit I wanted comfort, and I'd sooner have my whiskers fall off than admit I wanted comfort from *him*. Maybe I should lie down and attempt to get some sleep. We weren't going anywhere while it stormed outside. Thunder boomed in the sky, and I curled up into a tight, shivering ball. It was fine. I'd be *fine*. A bolt of lightning exploded outside the cave, and I jumped to my paws, heart ready to beat out of me. It wouldn't hurt if I slept a little closer to Grimm. It didn't mean anything.

I inched closer and scrunched up my muzzle. He still smelled like dog, but at least he wasn't wet anymore. In fact, his dry fur looked kind of fluffy and soft. He was a gray wolf, but pale gray, like his hair in human form except for his ears, around his face, and neck. His paws and underside were white, and when the moonlight hit his fur just right, it glinted like silver. I supposed for a wolf, he was rather handsome and elegant. His size should have frightened me, but I wasn't afraid of Grimm. He might be annoying, but he was good. Clearly the cold was messing with me if I was thinking Grimm was handsome and good.

Gingerly, I stepped closer. I reached out a paw and swatted at his tail before darting away. Nothing. Not an ear twitch. Hmm. Maybe he was a deep sleeper. I sat on my haunches to consider my options. There weren't many. I could curl up on my own—ignoring the perfectly good, fluffy, very warm bed right in front of me—and sleep on the hard, cold ground. Alone. The answer seemed obvious, but that answer also meant swallowing my pride. I was a prince. I shouldn't have to seek out a warm, fluffy bed. It should be offered graciously.

Okay, this sucked.

Screw it. I wanted the wolf pillow. Not *wanted* wanted. Only to sleep with. Ugh, sleep *on*. That wasn't any better. I was exhausted. No more thinking. I slowly edged closer, one step at a time. I'd sleep for a little while and wake up before he even knew I was there. Perfect. I was a *genius*.

Stepping carefully over his huge paws, I headed for the warmest spot, his belly. Unable to stop myself, I kneaded a little bit. Some instincts couldn't be helped. I made myself comfortable and settled down, curling into a ball against him, his body heat so good, enveloping me like a heated blanket. A purr escaped me, and I froze. I opened my eyes, relieved he didn't wake. The last thing I needed was him knowing he made me purr. Wait. No, *he* didn't. His fur did. That's it. I was using him for his fur. And warmth.

Eyes closed, I allowed myself to drift off, my purrs rumbling in my own ears. I could have sworn he moved, but I was too warm, too comfortable, and too sleepy to care. Once morning came, I'd simply deny anything he thought he saw or heard, and as prince, my word was law. Okay, maybe not law, but to be heeded.

Outside, thunder shook the world around us, and lightning set the sky ablaze, but I wasn't worried. I was safe here, with Grimm. As I sank deeper into blissful slumber, my last thoughts were of contentment and how I had never felt so at peace despite having no idea where I was or what would happen next. It was definitely the fur. Not the man. Nope. Not at all.

## CHAPTER FOUR

## GRIMM

NEVER IN ALL MY life had I known anyone more stubborn than the man in my arms. Despite how tired I'd been last night, I stayed awake in the hopes he'd come around. I'd curled up on myself and pretended to be asleep, knowing he'd rather freeze his tail off than come anywhere near me while I was awake. After what seemed a lifetime, he'd silently padded over, made sure I was asleep, then oh-so-carefully climbed up and made himself cozy. I hadn't been able to stop from opening one eye when I heard the distinct soft chainsaw-like purr. The joy that spread through me was ridiculous. I'd made him purr. The guy who would sooner claw my nose off than show any form of vulnerability around me.

In the months I'd been at his side, he'd never shown anything but frustration and annoyance toward me. He was convinced he didn't need anyone. My very presence insulted his princely sensibilities, which meant getting a rise out of him became my favorite hobby. Watching him lose his shit was so much fun.

Sometime during the night, we both shifted back into our human forms, and I woke up to an armful of reluctant prince. His soft snores made me smile, as did the jumbled mess of his hair. He had his arms tight around me, as if he were afraid I'd leave without him. His weight on me was heavenly, and when I inhaled his scent, I couldn't help the shiver that went through me. How could I be attracted to someone so... complicated? With a hum, he snuggled closer. He'd lose his mind when he woke up and found himself on me, but I was going to enjoy every second I could of him all soft and sleepy.

Light filtered into the cave, but the morning air had a chill to it. I didn't know what realm we were in. That seemed the only downside to the orbs. They appeared to take us where we needed to be but didn't tell us where that was. Enchanted forests were a dime a dozen. Every realm had one, or several dozen. *Contents may vary.* I snickered, and Owin let out a soft moan. Damn it, I hadn't meant to wake him. He lifted his head and looked around sleepily before his gaze landed on me. Slowly his eyes widened.

"Um, hello," he said quietly.

Taking a risk, I ran my fingers through his hair and smiled at him. "Hello."

"I'm lying on you."

"You are," I replied softly, afraid of spooking him.

"I... slept on you."

"You did."

Owin's gaze dropped to my lips, and my sense of self-preservation flew out the window. I pressed my lips to his, his surprised gasp allowing me to slip my tongue inside his mouth. The moan I let out at the taste of him was sinful. I'd never tasted anything so good. His lips were soft, his mouth hot, and the way he dove into the kiss had me wrapping my arms tighter around him. He slipped his fingers into my hair and closed them around fistfuls of it while deepening our kiss, his tongue trying to dominate mine. I drew my knee up between his legs, our very evident erections pressing against each other. His moan was decadent, and I couldn't help sliding one hand down to his rounded backside and giving a plump globe a squeeze, earning myself another delicious moan.

Forced to come up for air, he tore his lips away from mine and stared down at me, his breathing as unsteady as my own. "I... I kissed you."

"Technically I kissed you and you kissed me back, but yes."

"This can never happen again." His gaze dropped to my lips, and before I could reply, his lips were on mine. I slipped my fingers into his hair, and he shook his head and pulled back. "No. Nope. Not happening." One more kiss to my lips, then a frustrated groan. "Ugh, you're reprehensible." Another kiss. "So annoying!" Kiss.

I wasn't entirely sure what was happening, but I wasn't about to complain.

"Oh my Goddess!"

And there it was.

I'd expected the freak-out sooner, so I was prepared for it. Slowly I moved my hands off him and laid my arms to my sides. No sudden movements. I didn't trust him not to knee me in my boys, to be honest.

"Oh my Goddess!" He scrambled off me, and I was relieved his first instinct hadn't been to cause me physical pain. He sat, his hands in his hair.

"It's okay. Take your time."

"Don't you—*ugh*! I can't believe I—I can't believe we—" He clamped his mouth shut and shook his head, his fingers going to his lips.

It hurt that he immediately regretted kissing me. He'd enjoyed it. That much was obvious. Not even he could deny that.

"It's okay," I said softly.

"No, it's not okay," he said, his expression almost tortured. "I kissed a... a...."

"Bodyguard? Dog?"

"Wolf," he corrected quietly.

"I'm sorry?"

"You're a wolf." He dropped his gaze to his fingers. "I'm sorry for calling you a dog."

I shrugged. "Dogs are great. I don't take it as an insult."

"But I meant it as an insult."

"I know, but I chose not to see it that way." I concealed my smile at his pout. He looked so miserable. His expression quickly turned wary as he regarded me.

"Why are you so good to me?"

"I don't know that—"

"No. You are."

"Oh." I cleared my throat. "I like you." Why hide it? Besides, I'd been the one to kiss him, to make the first move.

"*Why?*"

He seemed so surprised by my response that I couldn't help but chuckle. "You really are adorable."

"And that's why you like me?"

"Why does that bother you?"

"Because that's what every guy wants to hear. That he's adorable. Like a puppy or those tiny versions of themselves humans are so obsessed with."

"You mean babies?" He really was too cute.

He waved a hand in dismissal. "Yes, sure, babies. Whatever. Either way, not a compliment."

"When I say adorable, I mean more along the lines of charming." I crawled closer to him. "Someone who inspires joy within me. Who makes me smile." Another crawl closer. "Makes me feel affection." I leaned into him. "Among other things."

"Right, well, um, as lovely as that sentiment is, I'm—"

"A prince." I sighed and sat back. "I know." We weren't as mismatched as he thought we were. I was an alpha, and as a monarchy pack, my pack was big, really big, and powerful. My family history went back to the old days, one of the very first wolf packs King Alarick had created. My position was on par with a prince. I simply didn't have a regal title yet, but that wasn't how he saw me. He shivered, and I reached into one of my pockets and pulled out a pair of warm socks. I handed it to him, and he stared up at me. "I know how much you hate it when your feet are cold."

"Thank you," he murmured, taking them from me. "I'm hungry."

The pout was out in full force, and I was a sucker for it. "I'll hunt you down some breakfast."

"I wasn't aware you could hunt scrambled eggs."

It was going to be one of *those* mornings.

"You need meat," I said, leaving the cave. Outside was beautiful, the sun shining through the trees, birds singing merrily. As suspected, we were in another forest. We could have been anywhere, from England to Yellowstone National Park, for all I knew. He followed me out, and I was aware of his eyes on me as I stretched. I may have flexed a little for his benefit, then pretended I hadn't heard his whimper.

With a big smile, I turned to face him. "Okay, so what'll it be? Rabbit? Quail? Boar? The menu will depend on our location obviously."

Owin seemed to think about it. "I'll have some scrambled eggs—soft scrambled, please—with some bacon, lightly buttered toast, and some sausage links."

"Even if I could get eggs and bacon, where exactly am I supposed to get lightly buttered toast from?"

He made a sound of disgust, very unbecoming of a prince, and flopped his hand in my general direction. "That's what your purse is for."

Did I say he was cute? What I meant was pain in my ass. "First of all, it's a satchel. Pretty sure I've mentioned that, like, a million times. Second of all, the magic *satchel* is to help us on our journey, not provide you with room service."

Owin shrugged. "Well, we won't know until you try, will we?"

*Patience.* The king would not be pleased with me if I returned without Owin. Or would he? No. *Opening a portal and pushing his Royal Highness through it would be bad, Grimm. Bad wolf.* I reached into the satchel and let it decide what I wanted, since I was torn between feeding Owin and dropkicking him. A handle of something heavy fit against my palm. "Wonderful. Just what I've always wanted," I muttered, removing the object from the satchel. "A cast-iron skillet."

Owin clapped gleefully. "Breakfast it is." He walked over to a moss-covered boulder, brushed some dirt off, then delicately dropped his butt onto it. "Don't forget the *lightly* buttered toast."

I was going to *lightly* hit him with this skillet in a minute. Well, I was kind of starving anyway, so I might as well make us both breakfast. The satchel provided all the ingredients, thankfully, because I had no idea where I would have gotten coffee from in the middle of the woods, and quite frankly, the caffeine was sorely needed before I could deal with Owin for what came next.

Breakfast was surprisingly pleasant. I made a fire and cooked for us. The satchel provided plates and cutlery. I had napkins in one of my pockets, along with seasoning packets. I got a weird look from Owin, but I ignored it. There was nothing wrong with being prepared. Once we were done, I washed up our dishes and cutlery by the picturesque lake, then returned them to my satchel, wondering where everything ended up. Finished, I turned and froze to the spot.

"What are you doing?"

He paused in the middle of removing his shirt to blink at me. "I'm going to take a bath. I slept in a cave last night, Grimm. Hence the smell of wet moss and...."

I waited for him to say "wet dog," but was pleasantly surprised when he didn't. Any response I had was carried off by the cool breeze as his unbuttoned shirt floated to the ground. He was lean, but every muscle was toned and sculpted, his waist trim. *Beautiful* was the word I was searching for. I'd expected him to shout at me to turn around or look away, but he didn't. He wasn't the least bit concerned with my presence, or my gawking.

"Would you mind seeing if there's a towel in your—"

"Satchel," I prompted.

"Purse," he corrected. "And some bodywash. Let's go with, bergamot. Oh, and a pouf, please."

I narrowed my eyes at him as I reached into my satchel. There was no way—

*Damn it all!*

He smiled knowingly. Apparently my desire was to give him *everything he* wanted. With a little saunter, he walked over to me and plucked the bath towel and small toiletry bag —yeah, I had it *that* bad—from my hand. As he stepped past, his devilish smile went straight to my groin.

"I'm going to finish undressing now," he called out behind me.

I lifted my gaze to the heavens and asked the Goddess to grant me patience. So much patience. Like, she'd have to borrow all the patience from lots of other people to give to me, because that's how much patience I needed right now.

"You should take a bath too. Not now, obviously, because I'm in the water. Naked. Completely naked. Not a stitch of clothing. My bottom is very bare right now."

"Yeah, I get it! I know what naked means, Owin. Thank you." Why me?

"Just saying. I wouldn't want you trying to sneak a peek at my princely privates."

Zeus strike me down right now. There was some splashing around, and I inhaled deep through my nose and exhaled through my mouth several times. My job was to guard his body, not to do deliciously naughty things to it. No matter how tempting.

"Oh dear! It would appear I dropped my towel whilst drying myself."

For the love of—I had to save my sanity whilst I still had the chance. *While* I still had the chance. *While.* I was losing it. "I'm going for a walk."

I didn't wait for a reply, just stomped off toward the trees. Was he laughing? You know, it would serve him right if I turned around, marched right over to him, and kissed him while he was naked. That'd show him. What it would show him was beyond me. I stilled. Wait. Why was *he* getting under *my* skin? When the hell had the tables turned? Was I asleep for it?

"I don't suppose you have a chocolate bar?"

I admit, my reaction was not very bodyguard-like. The fact he managed to sneak up on me was embarrassing enough—no need to bring my high-pitched shriek into this.

"Weren't you drying off?" I could have sworn he was trying not to smile.

"I was, and I finished. About that chocolate bar?"

I reached into one of my pockets and pulled out his favorite kind. "Here."

"Thanks." He tore at the wrapper and nodded at me. "Aren't you going to bathe?"

"That depends." I eyed him warily. "What are you going to do while I bathe?"

He looked around, then pointed to a fallen log. "I'm going to sit there."

The log was near the lake. As in, right in front of it.

"And do what?"

He seemed confused. "Um, sit? Pretty sure I just told you."

"Sit and what?"

"Sit and eat my chocolate bar."

There was more to this; there had to be.

"And watch you."

"There it is. No, you're not going to watch me bathe."

"Why?"

"Because that's weird, that's why."

He hummed and cocked his head to one side. "Is it, though?"

"Yes! I didn't watch *you* bathe!"

"Well, whose fault is that?"

"Oh my Goddess, I can't even deal with you right now.

Go sit on that log, facing *away* from the lake, and wait until I'm done."

He rolled his eyes at me. "Fine. I didn't realize you were so shy." He went to the log and dropped down onto it.

"I'm not," I protested as I headed for the lake. Not trusting him, I undressed as quickly as I could and waded into the lake. The ridiculous part—and there were a lot of ridiculous parts in all this—was that I really wasn't shy. As a shifter, getting naked didn't bother me at all, and neither did being naked in front of others. It kind of went with the whole animal thing, despite the magic. Being naked in front of Owin was a whole other story. I had no idea why I suddenly felt so awkward and aware of my body.

*Really? You have* no *idea why you might be feeling aware of your body in front of Owin?*

My brain needed to shut up.

Done bathing, I checked that Owin still had his back turned before hurrying out of the water. Damn it, I should have gotten a towel before I went in.

"I gotta say, I'm impressed, and I'm rarely impressed."

"Sweet Samhain!" I jumped and covered my princely parts with the satchel. "What the hell, Owin?"

He stood before me, hands clasped in front of him like he was there to chat about the weather or spank me for getting out of line.

*I know which one I prefer. Not helpful.*

"Do you mind?" I asked.

"Not at all."

I waited.

And waited.

"Are you going to turn around?"

"Why?"

"You said you didn't mind!"

A shrug. "And I don't. I don't mind seeing all that." He motioned to my body. "It's very eye-pleasing, actually. Do you work out, or is this just part of being a wolf shifter, because I gotta say, I'm starting to see the appeal—"

"Turn around, Owin!"

"Fine. So touchy." He turned, and I pulled a towel out of the satchel.

Halfway through drying off, I glanced up and noticed he was fixing his hair. With a mirror. A mirror that he was using to sneak a peek at me. I tied the towel around my waist and marched over to him.

"Unbelievable." I snatched the mirror from him. "Where did you even get this?"

"Well, it was in my toiletry bag. The toiletry bag *you* gave me, so really this is your fault."

I had no words. Giving up, I handed him back the mirror. "Enjoy the show." Okay, so maybe I was a little gleeful that his eyes were following my every move like he wanted to pounce on me. Pretending he wasn't watching me, I dropped the towel, relishing in the gasp he let out. I bent at the waist to take hold of my boxer-briefs and gingerly pulled them up, followed by my pants. I left them undone while I pulled on one sock first, then the other, followed by my shirt. Once I had my boots on, I zipped up my pants and fastened my belt, slung the satchel over my head, and strutted over to him.

With a hum, I put my finger under his chin and closed his mouth. "Careful what you wish for, sweetheart. You might get it."

"I despise you," he hissed.

"The rocket in your pocket seems to like me fine, judging by the way it's saluting me right now." I waggled my eyebrows at him, chuckling at his horrified gasp as he covered his very evident erection. He let out a frustrated shriek and stomped off. "I enjoy these bonding moments," I called out after him, big smile on my face.

Balance had finally been restored, which was good because this next part was going to suck, and not the good kind of suck. The kind that involved a prickly prince, a bar, and a terrifying hellhound. Hmm, there was a joke in there somewhere. Whatever happened, hopefully it wouldn't mean us ending up in hell. This was the last time I listened to my father. Interspecies relations my ass.

# CHAPTER FIVE

## PRINCE OWIN

It took longer than expected for certain princely privates to calm down. I only had myself to blame, really. As adversaries went, I'd underestimated Grimm. He was crafty for a wolf. Anytime I thought I was in control of a situation, he would find a way to turn the tables on me. Which was awful. Terrible. Not exhilarating in the least. I'd certainly not met my match. My verbal sparring with him was simply a way to pass the time while I finished this absurd quest. I certainly wasn't wasting any time thinking about our kiss, or his arms wrapped around me, his hands all over me. His sinful body hadn't entered my mind even once. Nope. Not a second.

Upon my return, I found Grimm sitting at the base of a tree, eyes closed as if he were taking a nap. I took a moment to admire him—his long legs, tapered waist, and broad shoulders. He was frustratingly attractive with his chiseled features and tempting lips, which I knew from firsthand experience were soft. His silver eyes were always bright and intense, his matching hair fell rakishly over his brow. I dropped my gaze to his strong hands and long fingers. He was so very—

"Like what you see?"

Annoying. He was annoying.

"So, what now?" I asked, crossing my arms over my chest. I was *not* about to address his question.

"Now," he said, standing up, "we go back to Solomon."

"The *hellhound*? Are you insane? I'm pretty sure you were there when he shifted and a hound with *flames for eyes* chased us!"

"Owin, you can't continue your quest without Solomon's help."

Damn it. I hated when he was right, so I poked him in the chest. "Fine! But if he drags us off to hell and the humidity ruins my hair, I'm blaming *you*."

"And your hair being ruined is the most terrifying part of that scenario, is it?"

"Grimm, my silky hair and porcelain complexion aren't made for extreme weather conditions. That includes hell, Florida—though if it's August I might argue they are one and the same—and certain areas of Canada in the winter."

Grimm pressed his lips together in what seemed an effort to keep from laughing. Could he not see my distress?

"What kind of an example would I be setting for my people if I walked around with frizzy hair and split ends?"

"Okay." He took hold of my shoulders and met my gaze. "I'll be right by your side. I won't let anything happen to you. I swear it."

The conviction in his words had me swallowing hard. He meant it. Granted, his job was to protect me, but something in his eyes told me his promise had nothing to do with him fulfilling his duty. It did something funny to my stomach. That had been happening a little too often for my liking. Maybe all this nature didn't agree with me. I missed my palace, with its bright and airy rooms, gorgeous library, and beautiful tearoom. The way the sunlight came in through the many windows on a perfect sunny day was bliss. I missed shifting into my ocelot form and bounding through the gardens chasing squirrels and sleeping belly up in the shade.

I nodded, the lump in my throat keeping me from speaking. Was it possible I took certain things for granted? Like the smiling wolf standing before me. He'd been so patient with me since arriving at my home, putting up with my diva behavior.

"Good." Grimm reached into his purse and produced a glowing orb. He tossed it onto the grass in front of us, and I took a deep steady breath, then followed him through. We were back in the woods behind the bar, a dark tall figure looming ahead of us.

"Took you long enough."

I arched an eyebrow at the hellhound. What did Grimm say his name was? Salmon? Salmon Man? No, that wasn't right. Wait! Solomon. "Well, Solomon, if you—"

Grimm cleared his throat.

"I mean, um...." I took a deep breath. "If I hadn't acted like such a jerk, you wouldn't have chased us. I... apologize for my behavior. I didn't mean any disrespect."

Solomon seemed to mull it over, and just when I thought I'd pass out from holding my breath, he shrugged. "Apology accepted."

"Wonderful!" Finally, I was back in the game.

"But I'm afraid I don't have what you're looking for."

"I'm sorry?" Something in my voice—most likely panic from my sense of impending doom—had Grimm stepping up beside me, his hand on my shoulder. The gesture was comforting, as I imagined was his intention. I'd never admit it to him, but I was grateful for his presence.

"I don't have what you're looking for. You need to find El Cadejo."

I didn't know what that was, but I'd go out on a limb and say another canine. "Thank you."

"Sorry."

"It's okay," I said with a heavy sigh. Apparently I'd be spending the rest of my days on this blasted quest. "Sorry again, for earlier. I appreciate your help."

"Sure. Hey, at least you're not alone in this, huh?" Solomon nodded to Grimm, and I found myself smiling softly.

"You're right. I'm not alone." I patted Grimm's hand. "Let's go."

Solomon nodded to the bar behind him. "You want to come inside? Walt makes the best nachos around."

"Thanks," Grimm said. "We'd like that."

I blinked up at him. "We would?"

Grimm stepped in front of me and put his fingers to my chin, lifting my face so our gazes met. "We could use a little break from all this questing, don't you think? Some food, maybe a mai tai for you, a mojito for me?"

"I suppose." He was trying to distract me, and I appreciated it. Also, nachos sounded kind of yummy.

"Great," Solomon said. "My mate, Cody, is behind the bar. Drinks on me."

"Thank you for your hospitality," I said as we followed him across the parking lot to the bar. The closer we got, the louder the noise, but it didn't bother me. I'd seen places like this on TV, though they mostly belonged to humans. Stepping inside, I was surprised by the mix of humans and magical creatures chatting and laughing together, though it was obvious the majority of the humans in here had no idea they were surrounded by hellhounds.

"Your pack?" I asked.

Pride filled Solomon's dark eyes, and his chest puffed up a little as he looked around the room. "Yep." He pointed to the bar and the blond young man behind it.

"That's your mate?" I gasped. "But... he's human."

Solomon chuckled. He glanced at Grimm before moving his gaze back to me. "The universe has a way of knowing what we need even if we don't know it ourselves. Make yourself at home. That's Walt over there. He'll make you the best nachos you've ever had."

Before I could ask what he'd meant about the universe and what that had to do with Grimm, he excused himself. Solomon walked over to the window first to speak with Walt.

"He looks terrifying," I muttered.

"Well, he is the alpha of the hellhounds."

"No, I meant the cook."

"Oh." Grimm chuckled. He took my arm and led me to a table, where I sat down on the bench and scooted to the middle, assuming Grimm would sit across from me, but he didn't. He slid in beside me.

I shimmied over, feeling my face heat, especially as I could see Solomon from the corner of my eye behind the bar with his mate. He whispered something in Cody's ear that had him blushing and then playfully smacking Solomon's shoulder. Solomon laughed, then helped with drink orders. They looked so... happy. Was that what it was like to have a mate?

"What an odd match," I mused, watching the pair.

"That's love for you," Grimm replied softly. I glanced over at him. He had a sort of sappy smile on his face as he watched the two. I'd forgotten how important finding a mate was to canines. Not that it wasn't important to cat shifters. It just held a different meaning for canine shifters. They seemed to feel the pull for a mate so much deeper. Wars had been fought over canine mates. As a cat shifter, my goal for a mate entailed finding someone I could tolerate and not want to bite all the time.

A shadow loomed over us, and I pulled Grimm in front of me to shield me, making him laugh. I was the only cat in this place, and he was my bodyguard. Did he think I wouldn't use him as a shield? *Ugh*, so many hounds.

"Nachos?" Walt narrowed his eyes at me, and I ducked behind Grimm, whispering hoarsely.

"Don't let him steal my soul."

Grimm patted my hand, clearly humoring me. "Thank you, Walt. Don't mind him; he's a cat shifter."

Walt grunted, like that explained everything, before disappearing to the fiery depths from whence he came. My guess was the kitchen.

I sat back and punched Grimm in the arm, or at least attempted to from my awkward angle. "And what exactly is *that* supposed to mean? He's a cat shifter?"

Grimm pulled the nachos closer. "Nothing. I mean, it's a known fact that cats can be a little... intense."

I narrowed my eyes at him. "Intense?"

Grimm picked up a nacho chip, his eyes going wide. He was practically drooling. "Well, you don't see canines biting someone for no reason at all."

I took the chip from him, and he growled at me. "No. Bad wolf." I crunched down on the chip and moaned, my eyes all but rolling into the back of my head. "Oh my Goddess, these *are* the best nachos I've ever had!"

"You stole my nacho," Grimm said with a pout.

"There's a huge plate of them," I said through a mouthful. I chewed and swallowed before pulling the plate closer to me. "Also, these are to share."

He huffed and took another chip, eyeing me with such wariness I couldn't help but laugh.

"I'm not going to steal your nacho." I petted him, and he whimpered. Pretty sure he'd be wagging his tail if he were in his wolf form. It was kind of cute. Wait, no. Not cute. I pulled my hand away so fast I almost hit it on the edge of the table. Yep, I was a real smooth operator. What was I doing? I'd petted him. In *public*.

"Here you go," Solomon said, placing a tropical-looking drink in front of me, complete with cherry and umbrella. He had a smile on his face like he knew something I didn't. "One mai tai." In front of Grimm, he placed a fizzy clear soda-type drink. "One mojito."

I arched an eyebrow at Grimm. "You were serious about the mojito?"

Grimm shrugged and took a sip of his drink. "You're not the only one who doesn't like beer."

Solomon chuckled. "You two enjoy each other."

I stared at him. "I'm sorry?"

"I said you two enjoy." He pointed to the nachos. "The food. Enjoy the nachos."

Pretty sure that hadn't been what he'd said. I squinted at him, and he laughed before walking off. Hounds were so weird. With a shrug, I went back to enjoying the most delicious nachos ever. By the end, I was stuffed and so content I could purr. When we were done with our food and drinks,

Solomon walked us back out to the forest where we'd first met him.

"Thank you," Grimm told him, shaking his hand. "We needed that."

"If you ever want to visit, you know where to find us."

"Thank you," I said, turning toward the portal Grimm had tossed onto the grass. "He's not so scary."

Grimm shook his head and shushed me. "Just step through the portal, Owin."

I laughed, feeling better despite having to go on what I feared would be yet another wild-goose chase.

The forest we entered was dark, but the moonlight filtered through the treetops enough to light our way. Not that either of us would have any trouble seeing in the darkness. An ocean of stars danced across the azure sky, and I admired them as I strolled beside Grimm. Come to think of it, afternoon naps aside, I couldn't remember a time when I'd taken a moment to enjoy the beauty around me. Thinking back, I recalled every time Grimm had asked if I wanted to go for a walk. Shame flooded me, and I felt my cheeks burn. I'd refused out of petty spite. I stopped and turned to face him.

"You okay?" he asked, his eyes glowing brighter than the moon. I bet he had a long list of admirers back home.

"I'm sorry," I blurted.

He looked at me with bemusement. "What for?"

"For rudely dismissing every invitation from you to stroll through the gardens or the woods. You were being kind and sweet, and I was petty and childish and—" He kissed my cheek, and I froze.

"I accept your apology." He held his arm out to me. "How about we take a stroll now?"

I nodded and looped my arm with his. Where was this

sudden shyness coming from? Whatever it was, I wouldn't give it another thought. Heat radiated off Grimm, and I gravitated closer. We walked in companionable silence until I couldn't keep it in any longer.

"I'm not... keeping you, am I?"

"In what sense?"

How many ways were there? I refused to think on it. "Keeping you from someone special. Back home."

"Oh, um. No. There's no one special back home."

That surprised me. "Really? I would have thought someone in your position would have a mate already chosen, or at least several eligible candidates to pick from."

Grimm's smile gave away nothing, and my brain was on the verge of imploding, trying to figure out what it meant.

"No," he said finally. "As heir, I'm very fortunate. My father believes in every wolf finding their mate through love. Not every prince or alpha is of the same mind. I have friends whose mates were chosen for them, or who chose a mate out of obligation. It doesn't make for a happy wolf. When the time comes, I'll ask the man I love to be my mate."

A fierce sense of jealousy for a man who had yet to exist flooded through me. Ridiculous, really. Why hadn't I given this any thought before? Grimm had been at my side for months. Why did I care *now*?

"Thank you, for all this." I motioned at nothing in particular. How far would I have gotten without him? I'd probably have been dragged to one underworld or another, suffering bad hair for eternity or until King Alarick decided I'd suffered enough for my arrogance and stupidity.

"Wow. An apology *and* a thank-you in one night," Grimm said, his lips twitching with the obvious need to smile.

"I regret it already."

"No, you don't."

Did he ever get tired of being right? "Whatever. Don't get used to it."

"I would never." He put a hand to his heart, and I held back a smile.

"Where do you suppose we are?" I took in the woods around us. Nothing but trees and forest for miles. I sniffed the air but couldn't get anything more than the scent of greenery and small woodland creatures. "It's kind of quiet, isn't it?"

Grimm stopped and glanced around, his smile turning into a frown. "Strange."

"Do you think we're in the right place?" Usually whatever hound I was meant to see would have shown itself by now. My inner ocelot wasn't happy about this, and judging by Grimm's stillness, my guess was his inner wolf was just as unsettled.

"I have no idea. I've never traveled via magic portal before. I assumed it would take us to where we needed to go."

I couldn't help tightening my arm around his and taking a step closer. I wasn't a scaredy cat by any means, but we were in a dark forest who knew where, filled with who knew what. I didn't like it one bit. "So, um, what do you know about El Cadejo, other than the fact we're dealing with another hound?" I asked as I got us moving again. Maybe if we continued to walk, we'd end up where we were meant to be.

"How do you know it's another hound?"

I arched an eyebrow at him, and he laughed.

"Okay, yes. Another big hound. Or hounds."

"Why would King Alarick do this to me?" I asked, an

unfamiliar ache in my chest. Maybe we weren't close, but the king always had our best interest at heart. We were his children. Sort of.

"Do what? Send you on a quest filled with canines?" He eyed me. "You honestly don't know?"

I let out a resigned sigh. "Okay, yes, I can see why all the canines. He does have the most twisted sense of humor." I shook my head and worried my bottom lip.

Grimm stopped walking again to put a hand on my shoulder. "Talk to me. What's worrying you?"

"I meant, why would he do *this* to me?" I asked, pointing at the vast expanse of nothingness around us. "This wild-goose chase? How long will this go on? What if all this is simply a path to failure? King Alarick knows everything. What if he knows I'm not worthy?"

"Do *you* think you're not worthy?"

"No! I mean... I *am* worthy."

"You don't sound so sure."

Oh, he looked worried. No one had ever looked so concerned for me before. It was... nice. Though I shouldn't get used to it. Better to concentrate on the issue at hand. I was worthy, wasn't I? Maybe I'd been a jerk to my previous bodyguards and to Grimm, but that didn't make me an unworthy prince, did it? I cared for my people. For those who chose to live in the human world, I kept a close eye on them and made sure they weren't exposed or taken advantage of. Should they ever need help, I would be there.

Was it because I never concerned myself with anyone outside my realm? We ocelots liked to keep to ourselves, but then so did many of the big cat shifters. It was part of our nature. Cheetah shifters were different. They seemed to prefer the company of others, as did lion shifters, even if they pretended otherwise. Should I have been reaching out to my brethren? A shrill, blood-curdling scream pierced the air, startling me so badly I shifted on instinct and climbed Grimm like a tree. I meowed, and he held on tight to me as I trembled in his arms.

"It's okay," he cooed, petting me. "I'm here." A scratch behind the ear and he had me purring. This time, I didn't care if he heard me. Someone had clearly just been *murdered,* and I wanted all the comfort. From him. Only him. "I'm going to put you down so I can go investigate."

I hissed at him and his absurd suggestion. Did he not watch human horror movies? That's how they all started, with some pretty but foolish human going to "investigate." Anyone with any sense would run away fast. In fact, we should have been tossing an orb out and making a hasty retreat.

"It'll be fine."

Famous last words.

Grimm tried to pull me off him, but I had my claws firmly attached to the thick fabric of his shirt. I meowed my distress and disapproval of his ridiculous plan to leave me and go traipsing into the woods after murderers.

"Owin," he said with a soft laugh. "Come on. Someone might need help. I promise I'll be back." He detached one clawed paw from his person, then the other before placing me on the ground. I glared at him. "That's the most adorable death glare I have ever seen."

*You know what's not adorable? Getting* murdered!

"Be right back."

I hissed, but he ignored me. Stupid wolf. He was supposed to be guarding *me*. The moonlight hit his silver hair, making it seem to glow. His broad shoulders tapered down to his waist, and I tilted my head at the exceptional view of his ass. I bound forward, then stopped myself. What in the world was I doing following him? Sitting my kitty butt back down, I waited, tail twitching, ear twitching, and listened for murdering. Nothing. How long did he plan to stay out there? Without me?

"Owin!"

I jumped onto my paws, my fur standing on end at Grimm's distressed call. He was in trouble! I didn't think about it, just took off into the woods as fast as my paws could take me. He couldn't have gone too far. As soon as I rescued him, he was going to get a piece of my mind. How dare he put himself in danger like this? As if I didn't have enough stress! Didn't he know stress caused wrinkles? I sniffed the air, trying to catch his scent, but got nothing. Meowing as loud as I could, I paused to listen and hoped he heard me.

"Owin, help me!"

I took off again in the direction of his voice, leaping over logs, climbing over fallen trees, and crawling through bushes that dared block my path. Several low-hanging branches received a swipe of my claws. Nature needed to get out of my way. My heart pounded fiercely, and the more I ran, the more scared I became. What if I didn't reach him in time? What if I lost him... forever? My meow was panicked and shrill, my paws moving faster than I'd ever pushed myself. I had to find him. He was *my* wolf, not theirs. Wow, where did *that* come from? No time to dwell on it. All I knew was that my wolf was in danger and only *I* could save him.

## CHAPTER SIX

### GRIMM

"So weird."

I listened for any sign of whoever had screamed but heard nothing. Maybe this was one of those weird screaming forests? The fact that was a thing was terrifying on its own. Sniffing the air, I picked up nothing. No blood, no other magical creatures, no humans. The screams had stopped, and I worried that if someone had been in trouble, they were beyond my help now. Turning, I headed back to where I'd left Owin. I couldn't help but smile. He got scared, and his first instinct hadn't been to run off and climb a tree—it had been to climb *me*. As adorable as he'd been, my heart swelled that he'd come to me for comfort, to keep him safe. He hadn't thought about it or hesitated, just climbed into my arms.

"Don't worry, Owin. It was nothing," I said as I walked out into the clearing. My heart stuttered and a chill went up my spine. "Owin?" Lifting my gaze, I checked the trees in case he'd gotten frightened again, but I couldn't see him. Maybe he was hiding? Probably angry at me for leaving him. "Owin, you can come out now. I'm sorry I left you alone. Why don't you come on out and yell at me?"

Nothing.

The forest was still.

"Owin? This isn't funny. Please come out." I sniffed the air, following his scent. Thankfully, ocelots had a very strong, distinct scent, and although his had begun to fade, it lingered enough for me to follow. Why would he go into the woods? Shifting into my wolf form so I could make full use of my heightened senses, I followed his scent, relieved when it became strong the farther into the woods I went. My instincts were on high alert, and the fur on my back stood on end when I found the path Owin had taken. By the looks of it, he'd been running. I howled, hoping he'd hear me.

"Grimm! Help me!"

My ears perked up, and I turned my head in the direction of his voice, but something wasn't quite right. The scent I picked up was Owin's ocelot scent, not of him in his human form, and it led straight ahead, as did the very clear path he'd left in his haste. How was his voice coming from the east? Maybe Owin shifted back just to call out? But why? I'd hear him better if he yowled. I howled again.

"Grimm!"

Again from the east. I turned back to the path before me and hurried. Something was very wrong. I barked and howled, tearing down the path in the direction of Owin's scent, not his voice.

*Come on, Owin, answer me!*

I howled again, and this time I heard it. A faint meow that turned my blood to ice. Something was in the forest with us, something that could mimic a human voice. Only one creature came to mind, one that was part wolf, but it wasn't El Cadejo. It was far trickier. Why would the orb bring us here? We were nowhere near where El Cadejo lived. I didn't have time to think about it. I'd been lured away from Owin by the very beast I was certain had used my voice to trick Owin.

The wind whipped through my fur as I sped through the woods, following Owin's scent. It got stronger the closer I got. I came to a clearing and skidded to a halt, my heart about to be ripped from my chest. Part hyena, part wolf, with sharp teeth that stretched up the side of its face, the crocotta stood over a trembling Owin, who lay in the grass at its massive paws.

Snarling and growling, I bared my teeth. The crocotta lifted its head to glare at me and opened its mouth, a terrifying hyena-like laugh escaping it. I took a step forward when two more appeared, one to each side of the first one. Owin's terrified mew shook me to my core, and I closed my eyes, summoning the power of my wolf pack. Being of alpha blood, and heir to the Prince of All Wolf Shifters, I didn't merely have the power to lead. I had the power to call on the strength of every member of my pack. My body grew triple in size, and my eyes glowed blue when I opened them. I snapped my huge jaws at the crocotta in challenge. I would tear them apart with ease if they so much as breathed on Owin. The two who'd appeared flattened their ears, sniffed the air, then darted off, clearly not in the mood to die tonight. Too bad I couldn't say the same about the bastard who'd lured Owin away from me.

The crocotta opened its mouth when a hiss followed by a screeching yowl filled the air. Owin sprang up, both sets of claws and sharp little teeth digging into the crocotta's muzzle. The hideous noise it let out at being startled and bitten hurt my ears, but I ignored it, barking at Owin before I leaped. Owin released the crocotta and scrambled out of the way just before I landed on the beast, my jaws closing around its neck. My heavier weight forced it onto the ground. It snapped its jaws, twisting and writhing in an attempt to get me off. I was bigger, but the crocotta had far more teeth.

Owin shifted into his human form, skin covered in dirt, nicks, and scratches, which pissed me off even more. I shook my head, my teeth still on its neck. It would pay for hurting him.

"Grimm, wait! Don't kill him!"

*Him?* I paused and eyed Owin. Was he serious? The crocotta had been about to suck his soul out and feast on his body like a tasty snack, yet he didn't want me to kill it?

"I know what you're thinking, and you're right. He was going to kill me, but that's not his fault. I mean, we all serve a purpose, right? Like the Cù Sìth and the hellhounds. Granted, sometimes that purpose is terrifying and the stuff of nightmares, but we're all part of the same world. I don't know why we ended up in this horrible place, but don't... don't kill him. You're safe, I'm safe, and that's all that matters."

I eased my jaws off the crocotta, fangs bared as I growled in warning. Slowly I moved off it. It stayed low to the ground as I put myself between it and Owin, my gaze never leaving the crocotta's. Owin's hand on my head soothed me, but I didn't let my guard down. The crocotta pushed itself up and sat on its haunches before lowering its head. Then it turned and trotted off, disappearing into the shadows. Owin came to stand before me, his hands on my face as he smiled down at me.

"Thank the Goddess you're okay." He threw his arms around me, hugging me, and I wagged my tail in contentment. When he pulled back, he gasped. "I didn't know you had that kind of magic! I thought you were only a wolf shifter."

I cocked my head to one side and whined, making him laugh.

"Okay, not *just* a wolf shifter. I mean, your eyes are glowing, and you're, like, ginormous. My arms barely fit around your neck."

He wasn't wrong about my size, but he was also small. However, I wasn't about to burst his bubble that my towering over him was all on my end.

"Why aren't you shifting back?"

Because I needed time to redistribute all the power I'd drawn into me from my people, and it didn't leave as quickly as it came. I barked, and he nodded.

"Sure. I have no idea what you're trying to tell me, but whatever it is, I'm sure you have a good reason." His expression turned concerned. "If you can't shift, how are we supposed to get out of here?" He darted his gaze to the shadows where the crocotta had disappeared. "I'm not keen to find out how many friends he's got in there. Though now that you're here, I'm not about to let you out of my sight, so their little ventriloquist act isn't going to work."

I licked at his hand, and he absently scratched me behind the ear, the only sound around us coming from my tail thumping against the ground.

"Why would the orb bring us here? I don't understand."

Neither did I, but I had a feeling this wasn't where we'd find El Cadejo. Standing, I nudged at his arm with my nose, and he lifted it, smiling at me when I stuck my head under his arm. I started walking, and he followed me, one arm around me as we made our way back to where the portal had left us. By the time we'd reached that part of the woods, I was almost back to my normal size. Brushing off a fallen log, Owin sat, one leg crossed over the other, fingers laced on his knee as he waited patiently, and regally.

Hoping to speed up the process, I picked up a stick and trotted over to him. He stared at me.

"Are you…? Do you want to play fetch?"

I wagged my tail, and he laughed.

"Okay." He tossed the stick surprisingly far, and I gave chase, leaping over bushes and logs. Scooping up the stick, I darted back and dropped it on his lap. "Ew, wolf slobber."

With a whine, I urged him to hurry up and throw the stick.

"Yeah, yeah. So demanding." He pitched the stick again, and off I went. On the fourth toss, I was back to my normal size and was able to shift. With a skip in my step, I hurried back to him.

"It feels good to have thumbs again."

"Grimm!" Owin launched himself at me, and I caught him with a laugh. He hugged me tight, and I returned his embrace, letting my cheek rest against the top of his head. Did he know how tight he was squeezing me, or that I could tell how happy he was to see me?

"You were really worried about me, huh?"

"No," he mumbled, leaning away to brush some dust off my shirt. "You had the satchel. I didn't want to get stuck here."

He might have been a wee bit more convincing had he not looked so miserable or had a death grip on my arm.

"The satchel. Right." I brushed my fingers down his smooth jaw. "How silly of me to think you were worried about me because you cared."

"I wasn't," he protested softly. "And I don't."

"Mm-hmm." I leaned in and brushed my lips over his. "Me neither," I murmured. "Good thing neither of us were worried, nor care about the other. It's not like we took off the moment we knew the other was in danger."

"Grimm?" Owin hummed.

"Yes?"

"Shut up and kiss me."

"Yes, Your Highness." I brought him up hard against my body and kissed him, loving the feel of his smaller frame in my arms. Mostly I loved how enthusiastically he returned my kiss. Like he couldn't get enough of me. I certainly couldn't get enough of him, his scent, the taste of him, the feel of him. It was all driving me out of my mind. I'd never wanted anyone so desperately. "Owin." His name tumbled off my lips like a plea, a prayer.

"Yes," Owin said through a moan against my mouth before he started to tear at my clothes.

"Are you sure? Maybe we should wait. It could be all the adrenaline and death and—"

"And maybe I want you to fuck me until I forget my own name, Grimm!"

"Wow. Okay." I stopped kissing him long enough to reach into the satchel. We might not need condoms like humans, but we still needed lube. Pretty sure this wasn't the kind of supplies the king had in mind when he gifted me the satchel for this journey, but— "Well, look at that. Lube."

Owin squinted at it. "Is there a note tied to it?"

I turned the note around, my face flooded with heat. "Um, yep. It would seem so."

"What does it say?"

"Rooting for you. P.S. It's waterproof. Smooches."

Owin covered his face with his hands. "Oh my Goddess. Who's it from?"

"There's no name, but he stamped it with his personal royal seal, so...."

"Oh my Goddess! Has the man ever heard of subtlety?"

I barked out a laugh. "We're talking about the same king who redecorates his entire palace along with the palace grounds whenever something shiny catches his eye. Remember his peacock phase?"

Owin narrowed his eyes. "Ah yes. It's where I met my nemesis. Peter."

"Peter?"

"Who names a peacock Peter!"

His indignant ire had me coughing into my hand to keep from laughing. "I'm guessing you and Peter didn't get along?"

"Every time I stepped foot in the palace, he somehow knew I was there, stalked me, waited for the right moment to strike, and *bam*! I'd have an armful of screeching peacock trying to peck my eyes out! I had to shift just so I had a chance against him."

"That... that sounds about right." I pressed my lips together. It took everything I had, but all I could see was Owin fighting a peacock named Peter.

"Let it out before you hurt yourself," Owin muttered, crossing his arms over his chest.

Tears filled my eyes from the laughter, and I doubled over, unable to breathe. Only Owin would have a peacock for a nemesis.

"Can we forget about Peter and get back to you sexing me up?"

I wiped a tear from my eye and straightened. "Only if you stop saying his name. He paints a very vivid image."

"I think I'm back to loathing you." Owin made to go, and I caught his arm, turning him back to me.

"Aw, don't loathe me." I placed a soft kiss to his cheek. "Not when you were starting to like me."

"I never said that."

Another kiss to his jaw, and he melted a little.

"Okay, how about, just when you were starting to not loathe me so much."

He wrinkled his nose, and my heart skipped a beat. "I think I'm okay with that."

Damn but he was everything I never knew I wanted. With a kiss to his lips, I gently pulled him back into my arms, when a low growl from somewhere in the woods behind me reached my ears. I paused. "Was that you?"

His eyes were huge. "Nope."

"Maybe we should move this to a forest that's not filled with soul-eating hyena-wolves?"

"Yep." He nodded fervently. "Good idea. I second the motion."

Swiftly reaching into my satchel, I pulled out an orb and tossed it on the floor before hurrying Owin through.

"Oh, look," he said, his voice dripping with sarcasm as he motioned around him. "Another forest. Maybe, and this is just a suggestion, your brethren should consider living somewhere more... not horrifying."

I chuckled and took his hand in mine, thrilled he didn't pull away. "Not all of us canines live in forests. Besides, you have a forest around your palace."

"The key word being *around*. I don't live *in* the woods. I live in a structure. Like a civilized shifter."

Glancing around, I spotted a small lagoon half shrouded by lush greenery and willow trees. "Come on."

"Where are we going?"

"To get cleaned up."

"Oh?"

I smiled, waiting for him to catch my implication.

"*Oh.*"

There it was. "Yes, *oh.*" The lagoon was picturesque with its colorful flowers and weeping willow trees, but most importantly the trees offered some privacy should anyone come wandering. My guess was that we were very alone, but considering my plans for Owin, it was best to play it safe. I lifted the sweeping branches to one of the willows and turned him to face me.

"I'm sorry you were hurt trying to save me," I said, running a thumb over his cheek. They were barely scratches, what with our shifter healing, but still, my heart skipped a beat every time I thought about him rushing off to rescue me without a second thought to his own safety.

"I told you I was fierce."

"Forgive me for doubting you."

He placed his fingers to my waist and hummed. "I'll think about it."

"Thank you. Maybe while you consider it, I'll treat you like the beautiful, courageous, extraordinary prince you are."

His smile was stunning. "I will accept you lavishing me with your worship and affection."

I held back a smile. "Worship, huh?"

"I am a prince, after all."

"Of course." I slipped his shirt off his shoulders. "Well then, Prince Owin, allow me to worship you as you deserve." Lowering to my knees, I enjoyed the sound of his gasp, and the feel of his fingers in my hair as I removed his shoes, then unfastened his belt. The little noises he made as I undressed him sent a shiver up my spine. Once he stood naked before me, I leaned in and inhaled, his heady scent making my hands shake and my erection strain against my pants.

I stood and quickly undressed, aware of his eyes following my every move. The satchel provided me with a blanket and the gift of lube from our king. Setting that up, I stood and turned to face Owin. His tongue poked out to lick his bottom lip, and I groaned. I was all but ready to pounce on him and take him where he stood. Forcing my feral wolf back, I took hold of Owin's hand. This wasn't about my desires. It was about showing Owin how I felt about him, showing him what our life could be if he kept me. As ready as I was to make him my mate, the choice was out of my hands. I froze at the edge of the lake.

"Is everything okay?" Owin asked, one hand on my arm in concern.

I blinked and dropped my gaze to his. *My mate.* I was ready to claim him as my own. I swallowed hard and smiled, hoping my sadness didn't come through. Owin would never take me for his mate. He was an ocelot prince, and I'd yet to meet a cat shifter prince who'd taken a canine shifter for a mate.

"Everything's great," I lied, placing his fingers to my lips for a kiss. He eyed me but thankfully didn't question me. Lacing my fingers with his, I led him into the cool water. Night arrived unexpectedly, and Owin gasped as the forest around us lit up.

"Oh, Grimm, look!"

His excitement made me smile more than the gorgeous sight of the blooming illuminated flowers. Fireflies floated around us, the leaves of the many bushes and multicolored trees sparkling with light and color. It was truly enchanting. A glowing dragonfly zipped over my head, and I plunged beneath the water, my heart squeezing when Owin joined me. He pushed his lips to mine before popping back up to the surface. I followed him, managing to wipe water from my face before Owin threw his arms around my neck and kissed me. I lost myself in his kiss and the feel of his naked body against mine. For now, he wasn't a prince, and I wasn't a wolf. Our tongues tangled, fingers explored and caressed. I mapped out every inch of his body while savoring the taste of him. He jumped and wrapped his legs around me, his hard erection trapped between us.

Holding him to me, I walked out of the lagoon and carried him over to the blanket. I knelt with him as he placed sweet kisses all over my face. Laying him on the blanket, I followed him down, our mouths once again finding each other, like we couldn't breathe if we didn't have our lips together. I lay over him, mindful of my heavier weight, and released a groan when he wrapped his legs around me, pulling me down against him. He thrust his hips up, and I shivered.

"Owin." I wanted to give him a chance to back out of this. To stop before we crossed that line.

"Please, Grimm."

That was all I needed to hear.

# CHAPTER SEVEN

## GRIMM

"I'm right here, love. Right here."

The way Owin shivered in my arms when I called him "love" was everything. He might be able to hide his words of affection, but his body betrayed him with every whisper of my name.

"You're so beautiful." I trailed kisses down his neck to his collarbone, groaning at his fingers digging into my back. His skin was soft and smooth, and the more I tasted him, the more I wanted. I licked a trail to his right nipple. flicking my tongue against the pink nub and smiling when he let out a hiss and arched his back up. Lavishing attention on the sensitive spot, I moaned when he slipped his fingers into my hair. He grabbed fistfuls of it, hanging on tight as I moved lower down his body.

"Grimm," Owin pleaded, his panting breath and moans sounding heavenly to my ears. I committed to memory every inch of his body, using my fingers and mouth. I licked, kissed, sucked as I lay between his legs, and he let out a string of unprincely curses when I swallowed his cock down to the root. I held his hip down with one hand to keep him still as I worshiped him with my mouth. His whimpers and pleas added fuel to the fire raging inside me.

While I sucked and twirled my tongue around the rosy head, I wet my fingers. Gently, I pushed one finger against his entrance, groaning at his soft gasp as I breached him. I moved slow, careful, my eyes on his flushed face as I searched out his sweet spot.

"Oh Goddess!" Owin arched his back up off the blanket, and I pulled off him with a smile. "Oh... oh my."

The way he lit up, his expression of pure pleasure, filled my heart, and I removed my fingers. His disgruntled huff when I pulled back was sweet. I grabbed the lube and nearly dropped it when he took himself in hand and started pumping his cock. My moan was indecent, and I almost swallowed my tongue when he drew his knees up, putting himself on display for me.

"Hurry up, Grimm, or I'll have to finish the job myself."

I growled at him. So impatient. He laughed and continued to pleasure himself. Little shit. As breathtaking as the sight was, I wanted inside him, wanted to fill every inch of him, leave a part of myself in his gorgeous body, to mark him. Lubed up, I placed the tip of my cock to his entrance, kissing him breathless before carefully pushing in. I sank into him, withdrawing slightly before plunging in deeper until several excruciating moments later I was buried to the hilt.

"Oh my Goddess! Grimm. I need you to move."

"As you command, My Prince." I pulled almost all the way out, then snapped my hips forward, my groan drowned out by his shouting my name. He wrapped his legs around my waist and dug his fingers into my biceps. Sweat beaded my brow, every muscle in my body coiled tight as I drove myself into him over and over, pulling out, then plunging in. The inferno inside me roared to greater heights with each cry of my name, and my hips lost their rhythm as I chased my release.

"Grimm! Oh Goddess, I'm going to...."

"Do it, love. Come for me." I leaned into him, one hand gripping his thigh, the other his shoulder as my groin smacked against his ass. Nothing in my life had ever felt this good. I refused to think of what would come after and lost myself in this moment, in the noises he made, his beautiful face and parted plump lips. Whatever happened, I would never forget the look of desire in his radiant amber eyes, or how he lay bare beneath me, allowing me to see every vulnerable part of him.

Bringing our lips together, I swallowed his shout as he shot ribbons of come between us. Owin's nails dug into my shoulders, and I tumbled over the edge, my release slamming into me. It shook me down to my soul, and a howl tore from my throat. My inner wolf snarled at the thought of letting Owin go. It wanted me to claim him, to make him my mate. I filled his tight channel, leaving a part of myself behind. Too sensitive to keep going, I carefully pulled out. I remained where I was, lying over him, brow lowered to his shoulder. I smiled at his fingers in my hair, tenderly stroking. Was he aware of how heartbreakingly gentle he was with me sometimes? It struck me then, like a lightning bolt from Zeus's hand to my heart.

I was in love.

*Fuck.*

This wasn't supposed to happen. I only meant to have

fun. I'd never intended for my heart to get involved, never worried it would. I flopped onto my back and stared at the stars as my breath steadied, waiting to see what Owin would do next. To my surprise, he rolled toward me and snuggled up close, which spoke volumes, considering how sweaty I was and his aversion to stinky-ness. We lay in silence for so long that I wondered if Owin had fallen asleep.

"What comes next?" Owin asked softly.

"What would you like to happen next?" I braced myself. With Owin I never expected anything less than the unexpected.

"I don't know. This... has never happened to me before. I need some time to think about... everything."

"Whatever you need." I rolled onto my side to face him, hiding the flinch from the sting to my heart. Brushing my lips over his, I deepened our kiss, finding joy in the now, in case this time together like this was our last. When I pulled back, his brow creased with worry, and I hated that I was the cause of it. With a smile, I took his hand and brought it to my lips for a kiss. "We should get some rest. Who knows where this path will lead us?"

"Grimm...."

I shook my head and popped a kiss on his lips. "We have a quest to finish. Everything else can wait." He looked uncertain, but nodded, and I was grateful when he didn't try to argue. Instead he let me help him to his feet. I led him back to the lagoon, where we washed up, and I distracted him by doing what I did best—annoy him. We played in the water, and he chased me around the lake. He was a very good swimmer, but then many cat shifters were. By the end of our time in the lagoon, he was ready to strangle me with my satchel.

We didn't bother dressing. The night was beautiful, the cool breeze heavenly against our skin in the warm evening. The moon was huge and round in the sky, casting a bluish glow across everything. The satchel provided a blanket, and I took the lead, lying down first, pretending not to hold my breath as Owin stood mulling over what to do.

"Should I see if there's a second blanket?" I asked, not wanting to put pressure on him.

He shook his head and dropped down onto the blanket beside me, staying close to one edge, a small gap between our naked bodies. Lifting the other side of the blanket, I covered us both, then lay on my back, one hand behind my head as I closed my eyes. Pretending to fall asleep worked the last time, so I steadied my breath.

"I know you're awake," he murmured before snuggling in close to me.

I smiled but didn't respond. Instead I brought my arm around him and kissed the top of his head. For what seemed like hours, I stared up at the stars, enraptured by the way they sparkled like a million tiny fairies.

When my father had approached me with King Alarick's request, I never could have imagined where it would lead. Being the bodyguard to a cat shifter would be fun, and to a prissy prince, even better. The longer I spent around Owin, the more I could see through his catty exterior. There was something very special about him. His heart was bigger than he was, that was certain. He hid it well from me, or so he believed, but I saw it every time one of his subjects came to see him at the palace. The gentleness he used with them, his attentiveness and care.

"You think very loudly," Owin muttered.

I chuckled. "I'm sorry. I didn't mean to keep you up."

He grumbled something I couldn't quite make out, then

went quiet for a few heartbeats before speaking up. "Are you okay?"

"I'm fine. Thank you for your concern."

He propped himself on his elbow, his gorgeous amber eyes studying my face intently. This wasn't a time for words, so I lay there, my heart pounding in my ears as he tentatively reached out and ran a thumb over one of my eyebrows. He moved onto my cheek next.

"You're... very handsome," he said. His cheeks flushed, and he cleared his throat. "For a wolf, I mean."

"Thank you."

He worried his bottom lip before moving so he lay half on my chest, his chin propped on his fist. "What's it like to be a part of a pack?"

"Well, it's both amazing and at times exhausting. It's amazing because you're never alone, which is also the reason it can be exhausting. I love that I have a big family, a huge network of pack members who care about me and support me. No one wants for anything because we all help each other. Together we're a force to be reckoned with, and they give the royal family power when we need it."

"Is that what happened with the crocotta?"

I nodded. "I drew power from members of my pack. It usually comes quickly, but it takes a little longer to redistribute."

"And they just give it to you freely?"

"Yes." I absently ran my fingers through his hair. "They know we would never call upon it unless in a life-or-death situation. They've given us their trust, and I would never abuse that."

"I can't imagine having a family that big."

"It's... a challenge when everyone knows who you are

and your business. Tough to keep your personal life personal. But the good outweighs the bad. Always."

Owin ran his finger over my bottom lip. "I bet they're missing you."

"I'm sure they are." His pout was sweet, so I pulled him in for a kiss.

That night he gave himself to me without hesitation, and in return, I let him have my heart. There was no sense in keeping it now. It belonged to him.

In the morning we dressed and had breakfast before heading into the woods. I hoped this time we were on the right track. Why would the king lead us on such a wild chase, not to mention put our lives in danger with the crocotta? But I trusted our king, and whatever his intentions were for this strange and at times perilous quest, he had his reasons. I also trusted that we would survive our next encounter, considering who we were about to meet.

"Tell me about El Cadejo," Owin said from beside me.

"There are two types of El Cadejo. A white one and a black one. One of them is good. The other will induce insanity and kill you."

"Oh, lovely. So which is which?"

I shrugged. "Sometimes the white one is the good one, and sometimes it's the black one."

"So what you're telling me is there's a fifty-fifty chance we'll slip into insanity and be killed. Good to know."

His deadpan expression made me laugh. "But that means there's also a fifty-fifty chance we *won't* go crazy and be killed."

He narrowed his eyes at me. "Don't be that guy."

I laughed again and popped a kiss on his lips. Taking his hand, I motioned to the dense expanse of trees up ahead. "Come on. We don't find El Cadejo; it finds us."

"Even better," he muttered.

I turned and straightened his cute little bow tie, despite the fact it didn't need straightening. "Here's what we'll do. If something big moves in the shadows, you close your eyes."

He arched an eyebrow at me. "And what will *you* do."

"Deal with El Cadejo."

Judging by his murderous glare, that was the wrong answer.

"Clearly you've already gone insane if you think I'm going to let you face that terrifying murder dog on your own."

"Owin, you're a prince. Your people need you."

"And your people don't? What about your family? Your parents?" He opened his mouth like he was going to say something else but decided not to. I was taken aback by how indignant he was and had to press my lips together to keep from smiling when he poked me in the chest. "Whatever inane idea you might have about sacrificing yourself for me, get it out of your stubborn canine head right now. I won't allow it."

"Oh, is that so?"

"That's right. In fact, I order you not to sacrifice yourself."

"I'm not sure you understand how this whole body-guard thing works." I wanted to gather him in my arms, squeeze him tight, and kiss the breath out of him.

"I don't have to," he said smugly, arms folded over his chest.

"Let me guess, because you're a prince?"

He patted my chest and smiled. "See, now you're getting it."

"Okay," I said. Of course, I had no intention of doing as he ordered. It wasn't just my duty to protect Owin; it was my honor. As long as I had breath in my body, no harm would come to him.

We walked through the woods for what seemed like forever, the only indication we were in a different set of woods was that these trees were so tall, they seemed to reach the sky, and moss covered everything, from the path we were on to the rocks and trees. Tiny white seeds floated around us, making it appear to snow, and colorful glowing mushrooms popped up through the moss as we walked.

Owin's hand remained in mine, and I could tell my presence brought him comfort. For the first time since we started this journey, he appeared almost... content. At times he even had a little smile on his face, and I would have given anything to know what thoughts had caused such a smile. Not once did he get upset about facing another hound, how long the quest was taking, or how much he wanted to be home. He didn't complain about his shoes getting dirty or the state of his suit, which considering everything we'd been through looked great. I was certain a good deal of that was down to Owin and how I didn't think there would ever come a time where he didn't look beautiful to me. Goddess above, I had it bad. Were my siblings here, they'd have teased me mercilessly.

Something large and black moved in the shadows. On instinct, I grabbed Owin and pulled him into my arms facing away from the danger.

"Damn it, Grimm! What did I say?"

I ignored him and his attempts to free himself from my embrace. The shadow moved closer, and I was about to tell Owin to shift when the huge black hound showed itself, eyes glowing red as it slowly moved toward us. Considering I was still breathing, it was safe to assume that this time, the good El Cadejo was the black hound.

"Welcome, young prince," El Cadejo said, it's voice deep and booming.

I breathed a sigh of relief. Owin pushed against my chest, but I didn't budge. He lifted his gaze, and holy smokes was he angry. I brushed my fingers down his jaw, my words quiet between us.

"Owin, I can't let anything happen to you. My heart couldn't take it. So you'll just have to be mad at me."

His eyes widened, and his cheeks turned a pretty shade of pink. He nodded, and I released him. Standing close, I let him turn to face El Cadejo.

"Thank you for receiving me," Owin said with a regal bow of his head. "My quest has led me to you."

The hound lowered its head in return. "I have been informed by your king. He is wise and noble, yet I do not have what you seek."

The disappointment that crossed Owin's face squeezed my heart, but I was proud of him for taking the news so well. He smiled politely. "Thank you. Do you know where I'm to go next?"

"Fear not, young prince. Your journey soon comes to an end, but be warned, not all is as it seems."

"What do you mean?"

El Cadejo bowed its head once more before disappearing into the woods. Owin turned to me, his expression one of concern. "Well, that didn't sound ominous at all." He took my hand in his this time and sighed. "Lead the way, then. Hopefully the orb won't drop us off a cliff or anything."

"That's the spirit," I teased.

"Shut up and give me a chocolate bar."

I pulled away from him and motioned to my many pockets. "You'll need to find it."

"Why is everything I need in your pants!"

"Really?" I waggled my eyebrows. "Tell me more."

"You know what I mean." His put-upon sigh had me laughing.

"Do I?" With every step he took toward me, I took two steps back.

"You're impossible."

"And you love it. Admit it."

"I will do no such thing. Now give me my chocolate bar before I bite you."

"Is that a promise?"

He lunged at me, and I took off, laughing as I ran ahead of him. I slowed down so as not to leave him too far behind. He cursed my long legs, and I brought his wrath upon me by telling him how cute his short little legs were. Shifting, he scrambled up a tree and became one with the branches and leaves.

"Aw, come on. Don't be mad." I stood at the base of the tree, hands on my hips. "I was only teasing."

A screeched battle cry of a meow and suddenly I had a fully-grown ocelot on my head.

"That's very mature," I muttered, receiving a whack in the face from his tail. Thankfully, he seemed to find jumping on my head amusing and didn't use his claws. He maneuvered himself so he was facing forward, and he smacked me on the nose with one paw. "Oh, I see. I'm your new mode of transportation, am I? We wouldn't want you dirtying your princely paws." He bopped me on the nose again, and I laughed. "Your toe beans are so cute!"

He hissed in protest, and I laughed. I reached into my satchel and removed an orb.

"Well, here goes everything."

# CHAPTER EIGHT

## PRINCE OWIN

Too stunned to meow in protest, I let Grimm lift me off his head and place me on the marble tiled floor. I quickly shifted and stood in stunned silence at his side.

"Are we...? Is this a palace?" Grimm whispered.

I only nodded, afraid to speak in case it was all some elaborate mirage that would disappear at any moment, revealing that we were actually in yet another forest. If that happened, I was going to lose it. Goddess above, it felt so good to have a floor and walls and a ceiling. A door opened and closed somewhere behind us, and we turned to see an elegant woman dressed in a white blouse and white pencil skirt approaching. Her blond hair was tied in a neat bun on her head, her smile friendly when she stopped in front of us.

"Prince Owin and Grimmwolf of the Grimm Wolves, welcome to the final stop of your quest."

My relief was instant, and I all but slumped against

Grimm. Thank goodness! I smiled up at him, startled by the sadness in his eyes. Why wasn't he ecstatic? We were almost done!

"Your host will call upon you tomorrow. Meanwhile, allow me to show you to your room. It's been a long and arduous journey for you. Bathe, eat, rest."

"Thank you." I took Grimm's hand in mine and followed the nice lady down the long, expansive corridor of white and silver marble. Beautiful paintings of flowers hung on the walls, and plinths displaying various vases of flowers and statues lined the hall, but nothing gave me a clue as to whom all this lavishness belonged. "I'm sorry, I didn't get your name," I said to her.

"My name is Irene. Anything you wish, you have but to ask."

"Thank you, Irene." I discreetly sniffed the air, not surprised to find Irene was a wolf shifter. Grimm didn't seem to know her, and he still looked worried. When we reached the room, Irene opened the door for us. "Thank you." I walked in, ready to ask Grimm what had him so grumpy when I spotted the huge bed.

"A bed!" I darted across the room and dove onto it. Smiling at Grimm's soft laugh, I rolled around on the plush comforter. Irene closed the door behind him, and I hugged a plump pillow close to me, inhaling the subtle scent of lavender and freshly washed cotton. The mattress was so soft and comfortable. I sat up, wondering why Grimm wasn't as excited as I was. "Grimm." I motioned to the bed. "A bed. An actual bed. Not just any bed, a massive one that feels like angel wings."

"It looks amazing."

"It *feels* amazing."

"I believe you."

I cocked my head to one side and studied him. "Why aren't you happy about this? Get on the bed. It's huge!"

He scratched at his jaw. "Do you want me on the bed?"

I blinked at him, confused. Why wouldn't I want him on the bed? I'd just told him to get on it. Wolves were so confusing.

"There's one bed, Owin. We'd be sharing. Do you want me to share a bed with you?"

My heart stuttered to a stop. Share a bed? That was very different from sleeping together in a cave or under the stars. The severity of the situation hit me. "Oh."

"Yes. Oh. It's okay." He pointed behind him to a chaise. "It's fine. I can sleep there."

The chaise wasn't nearly big enough for him or his long legs.

"Or I can just shift and sleep on the floor."

I gasped, horrified. "You're not sleeping on the floor."

He looked puzzled. "I did it every night back at the palace."

"What?" I scrambled off the bed, got tangled in the blanket, and nearly kissed the floor. Grimm caught me, like he always did, and placed me gently back on my feet. I grabbed his arms to keep him from going anywhere. "What do you mean you slept on the floor every night back at the palace? You had a bedroom!"

"Which is very kind, and I appreciate it, but my duty is to protect you." He averted his gaze and scratched himself behind the ear. "Every night after you went to bed, I shifted into my wolf form and slept outside your door."

And just like that, tears filled my eyes, despite how hilarious his panicked expression was.

"Owin? What's wrong. Why are you leaking from your eyes?"

I wiped the tears away. "You're so annoying," I said through a laugh. He produced a packet of tissues from his pocket and pulled one out for me.

"Here."

"Thank you." I took the tissue from him and blew my nose, my heart thumping wildly as he dried my cheeks. "I can't believe you did that. Why would you do that? And don't say it was your duty. Your bedroom was next to mine."

Grimm took my hand and led me over to the bed. He sat at the foot of it, drawing me to stand between his legs. His smile was beautiful, and I melted a little.

"I know this is going to sound crazy, and cheesy, but from the moment I saw you, this profound sense of protectiveness came over me. I didn't know why, but I knew I would do anything to keep you safe. You needed me, and not because you are smaller than me or weaker, because Goddess knows, you may be small but you are *fierce*."

I donned my snootiest voice. "As I've been telling you since the beginning."

His eyes sparkled, and for the first time in my life, I didn't feel fierce. I was scared. Afraid of losing him. Of what my heart kept trying to tell me whenever he smiled at me or teased me or put his hands on me, kissed me.... I swallowed hard and closed my eyes in an attempt to summon up some courage.

"When we return, I expect you to make other sleeping arrangements."

"Oh?"

"Yes. A perfectly good bedroom is going to waste."

"You do have several bedrooms."

I narrowed my eyes at him. "Not the point, Grimm."

"Right. Sorry. What do you suggest?"

*Come now. You're a prince!* I'd never had trouble stating

my mind. "Seeing as how you're protecting me, perhaps we make things easier for the both of us and simply... move you into my room."

"That *would* make things easier for the both of us, wouldn't it?" He pursed his lips in thought, and I was going to murder him if he didn't say something soon. "But I wouldn't want to impose. I mean, where would I sleep?"

"In a bed," I muttered, brushing some nonexistent fluff off his sleeve.

"Oh, are you bringing in another bed? I suppose your bedroom does have plenty of room."

"In my bed, Grimm! I want you to sleep in my bed with me!"

"There it is."

"Ugh! You are so frustrating!"

"And you're—"

"Don't you say it," I warned him.

He chuckled and brought me in close. "I was only going to say adorable."

"I'm going to throttle you."

"And I'm going to kiss you."

"Fine," I said with a huff, allowing him to wrap his arms around me. I'd never known anyone so infuriating. I slipped my arms around his neck as he pressed his lips to mine and kissed me. I melted into his embrace, parted my lips, and welcomed his tongue in my mouth. Kissing him was addictive, like catnip. I wanted to rub myself all over him and purr. How had we come to this? When did he gain the power to bring me to my knees? His smile had gone from annoying to disarming, his voice from grating to lulling, his presence from offending to necessary.

I took hold of the hem of his shirt and pulled it off him, then dropped it to the carpet, the need to feel his skin beneath my fingers consuming me. I'd never been so desperate for anyone's touch the way I was for his. Everything about Grimm confounded me, twisted me inside and out, and yet I needed more. *Wanted* more. I was consumed by my hunger for him. The idea of not having him at my side was something I couldn't entertain, and I was almost desperate in my need to get us naked.

Once I'd stripped him of every piece of clothing, I stood back and raked my gaze over his powerful frame. Every muscle was perfection, every inch of him mouthwatering. His hair fell over his brow, his eyes molten silver as he took in his fill of me in return.

"You're so beautiful, Owin."

I shook my head. Maybe I was pretty, but I'd been selfish, arrogant, and spoiled, while he was kind, loyal, and affectionate. He was beautiful inside and out. As I reached for him, he took my hand, and I pulled him with me onto the bed.

"Lie down."

As always, he did as I asked, lying on the bed, his hands behind his head. I straddled him and leaned in to kiss him, a quick but passionate kiss that hinted of things to come. This time, *I* wanted to make *him* feel good.

"It's my turn to worship you," I told him, smiling at his sharp intake of breath and the way his pupils dilated. He lay before me, a delicious treat for me to savor, and I had every intention of taking my time, of tasting every inch of him. I climbed off the bed and grabbed his satchel. With a laugh, he took it from me and reached into it, waggling his eyebrows when he pulled out yet another bottle of lube. Dropping the satchel off the side of the bed, he checked the note attached—because of course there was a note attached —and groaned.

"What does it say?" I asked, straddling his lap again. Judging by his reddened face, maybe I didn't want to know.

"This one's from Lord Eldrich."

"I can't believe he got Lord Eldrich involved."

"It says he's thrilled at how far we've come."

"Please tell me he didn't."

"He signed it 'pun intended.'"

"Oh Goddess." I covered my face with my hands. "Why are they so weird?"

Grimm shrugged. "Who knows? They're immortal."

I grabbed the lube from him and leaned in to kiss him. "We have lube, and that's all that matters."

"I like the way you think." He slid his hands down my sides and over my back to my ass. "What can I do for you, my Prince?"

I hummed in approval. "You can be a good little wolf and put your arms above your head."

"Yes, My Prince."

A little shiver went up my spine at the sight of him surrendering so completely. He did as I asked, placing his arms above his head and exposing his neck to me. I drew in a sharp breath at the gesture, knowing what it meant to him and his kind. Placing a kiss to his neck, I rewarded him for his valor by palming his erection. The whimper he let out made me painfully hard. I used the pearls of precome on the rosy tip of his cock to ease the friction as I slowly pumped his rock-hard shaft. He writhed beneath me but didn't try to touch me.

"Such a good boy," I murmured before sucking his earlobe into my mouth. He snapped his hips up in response, and I smiled before nipping at his jaw. I maneuvered myself between his legs. "Knees up." With a delicious groan, he bent his knees, and I pushed his heels closer to his body so I had better access to his puckered entrance.

"Oh Goddess, *Owin!*" Grimm all but flew off the bed when I tasted his hole.

How had I not known how thrilling it could be to give someone else pleasure? How heady the feeling of having someone desire you to the point they trembled at your touch? Every labored breath, every moan and gasp was for me, *because* of me. I'd never had such an effect on anyone, but most of all, I loved that I had this effect on Grimm. He grabbed fistfuls of the comforter, his head thrown back and his toes curled.

"Please let me touch myself."

I speared him with my tongue, and he cried out my name. If I didn't calm myself, I'd come there and then. I took a steading breath and lifted my gaze to his. His eyes were so beautiful—thin silver rims around pitch-black. I nodded, and he didn't waste a moment in palming his cock. His groan sent a shiver through me. He was all but ready to come apart in my hands. Never had I been this intimate with anyone, nor had I ever wanted to hold on to them after.

"I want you, Grimm."

"Yes. Take me. Take anything you want."

I crawled over him, my gaze locked on his. "No, I want *you*, Grimm. I want to keep you. I want you at my side. Not as my bodyguard, as... my mate."

His lips parted in a silent gasp, and his eyes grew glassy. His smile was the most beautiful thing I'd seen in my life, and my heart all but beat out of my chest. We'd have so much to figure out, but I didn't care. As long as we were together, we could do anything.

"I can't imagine my life without you, Grimm." I let my

brow rest against his, emotions I'd never felt before swirling around inside me like a storm.

"Owin," he whispered, and I opened my eyes. He turned his face, baring his neck to me, and I stopped breathing.

My title of prince declared me nobility, of royal blood. A certain amount of power came with that title, as did expectations and responsibilities. I was strong, resilient, and a fighter. But I was not an alpha.

Grimm's title stated what he was inside, in his blood, his bones. He was a natural-born leader, his body and spirit strong enough to not only draw power from his people but keep it within himself and use it. Grimm possessed a strength beyond what I had seen, and yet here he was submitting to *my* bite. My heart pounded in my ears, and I blinked back my tears. I didn't need to be a canine to understand the seriousness of his gesture.

"Are you sure?"

He turned his head to face me, his smile warm and his eyes filled with an emotion I was terrified he would voice. Mating was powerful enough without bringing *that* into it.

"I've never been surer, My Prince." He ran his fingers through my hair, then down my jaw. "Owin."

I turned my head to kiss his fingertips. "Okay." Taking a deep breath, I waited for him to bare his neck once more. When he did, my fangs grew out and I leaned in to lick the soft spot between his neck and shoulder. He hissed when my teeth pierced his skin, his fingers tightening on my hips. Our blood bonded, and a spark of blue exploded in front of my vision, heat flooding through me from my head to my toes. My vision sharpened, and I released him. He drew in a sharp breath, back arching up off the bed, before he settled, eyes closed.

"Grimm?" I asked softly, petting his head. "Are you all right?"

He opened his eyes, and they glowed blue. A wicked smile played on his lips. "My turn." The deep huskiness of his voice resonated within me, and I trembled. I let out a squeak when he bounded up and wrapped an arm around me, and I laughed when he turned us so I was underneath him.

"Oh my."

He licked a trail up my jaw and nipped at my earlobe. "Do you want to see how an alpha does it?"

I nodded fervently. "Yes, please!"

He took hold of my chin, his gaze intense. "It *will* change you, Owin. A part of me will forever belong to you. My power will belong to you."

I stared at him. "What?"

"As my mate, you'll be able to call on my power should you need it. That's how strong our connection will be. Tell me this is what you want."

"I want this." I took his hand and kissed it. "I'll make you proud."

"You already do." With a playful snarl that made me laugh again, he turned me onto my stomach. I gasped when he lifted me onto my hands and knees. I heard the lube cap open and shut, then a cool finger breached my hole.

"Grimm!"

He made quick work of stretching me, his finger hitting that sweet spot over and over. By the time he finished, my legs were shaking. He positioned himself above me, his chest to my back, and one arm around me.

"Owin?"

"Yes?"

"Prepare yourself."

Before I could make a snarky comment, he plunged inside me, and I screamed his name. A sharp pain pierced my shoulder the moment his fangs did, but I didn't have time to think about the pain when he snapped his hips.

"Oh, sweet Mother Goddess! *Yes!*"

My entire body thrummed with a blue light I couldn't see but I could *feel* coursing through every inch of me. A fiery heat exploded through me, and I cried out, the room bursting with blue light that seemed to have come from inside me. I'd never felt anything like it, as if his alpha power was rushing through every part of me. It was both terrifying and exhilarating. I closed my eyes and allowed his power to consume me. He moved wildly against me, his groin slamming into my ass over and over, thick, hard cock pounding into me. My limbs shook, but I remained firm as he made me his, claimed all that I was. My body, my mind, my soul... my heart. He was my mate, and I was his.

"Grimm," I pleaded, breathless.

His hips lost their rhythm as he drove himself deep inside me the way only an alpha could. If I didn't touch myself, I was going to explode. At least I thought so. With one final deep thrust, Grimm wrapped his hand around my cock and growled in my ear.

"Come."

"Grimm!" My release slammed into me with the force of an ocean wave crashing against a mountainside. Stars danced in front of my eyes as I came, my body shaking so hard I thought I would come apart. My insides burned as his release coated me, marking me his. No longer able to hold myself up, I collapsed onto the bed, with Grimm on top of me, our panting breaths the only sound in the room.

Pure bliss enveloped me, and I didn't so much as open

my eyes when he slid off me to lie beside me. I felt his fingers in my hair and his warm breath on my cheek.

"Are you all right?"

I grunted, receiving a chuckle in response.

"I'm going to take that as a yes." The bed dipped, and I felt him lean over me. "It's healed already."

"Less talky more nappy."

"Owin?"

"Clearly you aren't familiar with the concept of napping. We cat shifters love to nap."

"Yes, I know. I've watched you nap every afternoon for months."

"Not stalkery at all," I mumbled, ignoring his laugh.

"Owin."

Clearly he wasn't going to let me nap, so I opened my eyes. "Yes, Grimm?"

His grin was ridiculous. "We're mates now."

I narrowed my gaze at him. "I hope you don't think this means I'm going to be all lovey-dovey or something."

He threw his head back and laughed. I loved the sound, and I bit down on my bottom lip to stop from smiling, or at least attempted to.

"I wouldn't dream of it!" He placed his hand to my cheek. "Your eyes are blue."

"What?"

"It's only temporary. Once my powers settle inside you, your eyes will return to normal. Still cute, though."

Ugh, canines. Now he was all cheery and excited. "How are you not exhausted?"

He blinked at me and leaned in to boop his nose with mine. "Because I have a mate, and even if he is a grumpy kitty, I'm thrilled."

"You are never, *ever* allowed to call me a kitty again. Do you hear me?"

His eyes sparkled with mirth. "Got it. Hey, do you think it's weird that we just had sex in some stranger's bed?"

I stared at him before rolling onto my back and bursting into laughter. Oh my Goddess, my mate was so weird. I gasped and froze. I had a mate. A soft chuckle met my ear, and he leaned over me.

"There it is," Grimm said quietly before kissing me.

"So annoying." I wrapped my arms around him and kissed him back.

"And all yours."

I'd take it.

# CHAPTER NINE

## PRINCE OWIN

"I don't like this."

I didn't disagree with Grimm. Something wasn't right. This morning Irene woke us up and informed us our host was ready to greet us. We'd quickly dressed, then joined her outside where we followed her down several empty hallways, all of them identical to one another. She showed us into a strange room, then excused herself. A good deal of time later, and we were still waiting. Why hadn't our host shown themselves? I didn't understand why all the mystery. Despite the sunlight coming through the huge open windows, the expansive room was cold and empty. It reminded me of a mausoleum. A chill went up my spine, and I leaned into Grimm.

Grimm looked around, but there wasn't much to see. "It is kind of... sparse in here, isn't it?"

The gray stone floor was bare, as were the walls. It was void of any furniture or decor. If I'd been in my ocelot form, I was certain my fur would have been bristling.

"Maybe we should go." I turned toward the door, but Grimm gently pulled me back to him.

"We've come this far, Owin." His hand on my cheek settled my nerves, and I was so grateful he was here. So much so that....

"I'm glad you're here with me," I told him, squeezing his hand.

His smile was beautiful. "I'm glad I'm here with you as well."

"Welcome, my darlings."

Grimm jolted at the voice, and I wondered who on earth had the power to cause such a reaction in an alpha wolf as fearless as Grimm. He turned and gaped at the woman approaching.

"Mom?"

His *mother*? "*What?*"

"Hello, my love." She smiled at Grimm, her silver eyes filled with motherly adoration.

"Um, Owin, this is my mother, Louve. Mom, this is Prince Owin."

"It's so wonderful to finally meet you, Owin." She took my hands in hers and smiled warmly. "My, but you're prettier in person."

"Oh, um, thank you."

"Mom," Grimm said through a groan.

She chuckled, and I found myself smiling. Louve was a stunning woman, with long pale silver hair like Grimm's that cascaded over her shoulders. Her black-and-gray pencil dress was classy, and she was tall, nearly as tall as Grimm, even without the two-inch heels. Her pupils dilated, and she sniffed the air.

"Oh." She looked from Grimm to me and back.

"Yes," Grimm said, tucking me against his side. "I've found my mate."

Her eyes filled with tears, and she put a hand to her quivering lips. "Oh, baby. I'm so very happy for you." She threw her arms around us both and hugged us with a strength I never imagined her having. Went to show how much I knew about wolves. With a sniff, she pulled away and smoothed out her dress. "Your father will be so thrilled. Anyway...." She cleared her throat and turned to me. "Prince Owin, your journey has come to an end."

I could barely contain my excitement. "You have what I've been searching for?"

"I do."

"Yes! We did it!" I threw my arms up with a whoop before launching myself at Grimm. He caught me with a laugh and hugged me tight as I wrapped myself around him.

"We did, didn't we?" he said as he buried his face in my neck. Gently he put me down, and I found I didn't want to release him.

"Thank you, Grimm." I couldn't have done this without him. Finally we were going home. We could start our new lives together.

"You're welcome."

I turned and my heart skipped a beat. In her hands, Louve held an open velvet box, and nestled inside was the most glorious treasure I'd ever seen. My crown.

"Your prize, young prince."

I couldn't stop the tears from welling. Never again would I take my position for granted. I took a step forward, and Louve closed the box, her smile turning sad.

"There is, however, a price you must pay."

"A price?" Wait. What was happening right now. No one said anything about a price. I thought I was just supposed to reach the end.

"In exchange for your crown, you must make a sacrifice."

My heart stuttered. "What... um, what kind of sacrifice?" I stepped closer to Grimm, needing to feel his steady, unflappable presence. It would be okay. Everything would be okay as long as I had him by my side. Whatever the price, I would pay it. A huge green hound appeared from behind Louve, and I started to shake. Buried somewhere inside, in my deepest fears, I knew the price that would be asked, but I refused to believe it. The Cù Sìth sat beside her, its glowing red eyes on me.

"What... what is he doing here?" I asked her.

"You may take your crown, Prince Owin, but Grimm must stay."

"What do you mean?"

Grimm stepped in front of me, blocking my view of the Cù Sìth. He placed a hand to my cheek, his sad smile breaking my heart. "She means, the Cù Sìth will take me to the fae underworld."

"Oh my Goddess! That's a little harsh, don't you think?" I stepped out from behind Grimm. "You can't be serious."

"That is the price," she said, holding the box out to me.

"And if I don't take it?" I asked, stepping away as if the very nearness of the box might burn me.

"Then you fail in your quest."

"It's okay, Owin," Grimm said, lacing our fingers together.

"No, it's not okay." I turned to her, pleading. "This... this isn't fair."

"Life rarely is, my child."

"But I've proven myself. I reached the end."

"That was not your quest."

I didn't understand. "He's your son."

"And I love him with all my heart."

"How could the king do this?" No, I would not accept this. I was furious. "How could he—*why* would he?"

"You must make a choice," Louve said gently. "Your title or your companion."

"He's not my companion!" Both Louve and Grimm stared at me. "I'm sorry. I didn't mean to yell. Grimm is more than my companion. He's more than my bodyguard. Hell, he's more than my friend. He's my mate. What's more, I love him. I can't leave him behind." I shook my head, my fists at my sides. "I won't leave him behind." I turned to face the Cù Sìth and hissed, my claws extended. "And no one is going to take him away from me."

"Owin, stop and think a moment." Grimm cupped my face. "This is your quest. *The* quest. You can't forfeit everything just for me."

"Watch me."

"Love. Listen, please."

"I'm not leaving here without you, Grimm. Do you hear me? I love you. You changed my life. For months all I could think about was how to get rid of you. Do you know why?"

Grimm shook his head. "I figured it was because you hated me."

I withdrew my claws and cupped his face. *Silly wolf.* "I tried so hard to get you to go because I was terrified that if I didn't, I'd ask you to stay."

"What?"

"The moment you walked into my throne room, I was in trouble. I'd never been so drawn to someone I'd just met.

The longer you were around me, the more I got these silly ideas of us together. I've been hurt before. A lot." I let out a soft laugh. "It sounds stupid, but being a prince isn't easy, and if my own kind couldn't bear to stick around, what hope did I have with someone who didn't understand a cat shifter much less a prince? I did what I always do when I'm scared. I lashed out at you."

"Oh, Owin. You are the most amazing guy I have ever had the honor of knowing. I've loved you from the very first day you tried to push me off the bridge and into the lake. Wolves are very good swimmers, by the way."

I laughed through my tears. "So annoying."

"I know," he said, taking my hand and placing it to his lips for a kiss. "Which is why I think you know what you have to do."

I sighed and nodded. Kissing his cheek, I turned and stepped forward. Lifting my chin, I met Louve's gaze. "I have made my choice. King Alarick will have to find another prince to rule in my stead."

Louve pressed her lips together as if holding back a smile. "Owin, I will give you one more chance to complete your quest. Take the box."

"Thank you, but no, and you know how much we cats love boxes."

The room exploded with life, the sun shining through the windows, chasing the shadows away. Everything around us changed, and I quickly stepped back beside Grimm.

"Wait a second." I squinted around the room. "Is this...?"

"Congratulations, Owin! You've succeeded in your quest." King Alarick appeared on his throne, Lord Eldrich at his side.

"We were in your palace *the whole time*?" I gasped. Oh my Goddess, we had sex in one of the king's bedrooms!

With a booming laugh, he stood and motioned around us. "Neat trick, huh? Something I picked up from the fae many centuries ago."

My temper flared. I marched over to King Alarick and slapped him. Hard. "I can't believe you!"

"Ouch!" The king stared at me. "You slapped me." He glanced over at Lord Eldrich with a pout. "He slapped me."

Lord Eldrich merely shrugged, a smile on his face. "I told you it was a terrible idea."

"Thank you, Jean." The king wasn't impressed with his advisor's response. He turned back to me and arched an eyebrow.

Oh my Goddess, I'd just slapped the king!

"There it is," Grimm said with a chuckle as he stepped up beside me. I elbowed him in the ribs, making him laugh.

"Not helpful." I quickly dropped to one knee. "I am *so* sorry, Your Majesty."

"Get up, Owin. At least tell me *why* you slapped me."

Was he serious? I quickly stood. "You were going to send Grimm to the fae underworld!"

He blinked at me. "No, I wasn't."

"Fine, my selfishness would have sent him to the fae underworld, but either way, you were going to allow Grimm to be taken!"

"No, I wouldn't have."

Why was he so confounding! "I don't understand."

King Alarick smiled warmly and patted my cheek before returning to his throne and taking a seat. "Owin, I was never going to have Grimm sent to the fae underworld. I only needed *you* to believe he'd be taken there."

My jaw went slack. "It was a test?" Oh, he was sneaky.

"Yes. That's sort of what a quest is."

And a smartass. Definitely a wolf at heart.

"So... you were never going to let him get taken?"

"No."

There had to be more to this. "What if I'd chosen my crown?"

"You wouldn't have."

"How do you know?" I mean, immortals were pretty sure of themselves, but he couldn't have been *that* sure.

"Owin, the quest would have gone on for as long as it took for you to learn that your worth didn't lie with your title, but with your heart. You were good to your people, but not to yourself. You shielded your heart, believing you didn't need anyone, that *you* were the reason your suitors abandoned you. It's not enough for your people to need you and love you, Owin. You must need them and love them in return. You also needed to be humbled a little bit." He gave me a pointed look, and my face heated.

"The whole canine thing."

King Alarick nodded. "Yeah, the whole canine thing." He perked up and motioned to Grimm. "And look, now you've fallen in love with one."

"But wouldn't a worthy prince put his people before himself? I chose love over my crown."

"And if you will recall, I'm the one who chooses those worthy to rule. I would have found someone worthy to rule in your stead, but the love you've found in Grimm? No one could replace that, Owin. You made a great sacrifice for him." He turned to Louve. "Thank you for assisting."

"It's an honor, Your Majesty." Louve approached King Alarick and handed him my crown.

"Did you know about this?" Grimm asked his mother.

She smiled warmly at him. "I was summoned by our

king and informed of Owin's quest. I knew you wouldn't be taken to the underworld."

Which explained why she hadn't been distraught over it, but something still puzzled me. "Why did you look so sad, then?"

"I didn't know what your choice would be, and my son had taken you as his mate. He might not have faced the fae underworld, but I feared he might be facing a broken heart."

I took Grimm's hand in mine. "I promise to do everything in my power to protect his heart."

"You see," King Alarick said to Lord Eldrich. "I sent him on a quest to prove his worthiness, and not only does he succeed but comes back with a mate." He wiped at his eye. "They grow up so fast."

Lord Eldrich shook his head, his lips quirked in amusement.

"Step forward, Prince Owin of the Ocelot Shifters," the king said, his smile wide despite the command.

I did as he asked me, stepping before him. My pulse beat wildly, and I took a deep, steadying breath, then released it slowly as he placed the crown on my head. *My* crown. My bottom lip wobbled as I gazed up at him, the pride in his eyes filling me with joy. His eyes were still weird, though.

"I'm so very proud of you, Owin," he said as he brought me in for a hug. I clung to him, his words meaning more to me than he could ever imagine. "Go on now. Enjoy your new mate."

"Thank you." I joined Grimm, who stood with his mother, and I gave her a hug.

"We'll see you soon," King Alarick promised.

She nodded and took my hand before giving my cheek a kiss. "Welcome to the family, Owin."

The happiness her words instilled in me was unlike anything I'd ever felt. I had my parents, yes, and they adored me, but they were off on their adventures now that my father had retired and didn't have a realm to run. I thanked her, promised we would make a visit to her pack our first priority once Grimm was settled at my palace, and left the throne room.

Outside in the hall, I noticed Grimm still had the satchel. "Are we supposed to give it back?"

Grimm shook his head. "Nope. Lord Eldrich said it was my gift for the long and arduous journey."

"A little inconvenient maybe, but I wouldn't say arduous," I muttered.

He laughed and pulled me in for a kiss. "Yanking your tail."

Good thing he was cute. "Might I suggest you not yank a cat shifter's tail? That can only lead to bandages. Many bandages. Does this mean we can portal ourselves back to our palace?" A magic satchel with an endless supply of magic portals? I could barely contain my glee. I'd never again have to get up from my windowsill to get a snack. I could portal my snack in. The possibilities were endless!

"We're not using portals to get you snacks."

I peered at him. Damn it, I should have asked his mother if he was a seer wolf. He took my hand and led me down the hall.

"Still not a seer wolf. I pay very close attention to you."

"Stalk much?"

"All the time. You're very fun to stalk."

"Pft. We all know I'm the better stalker. Remember the time I jumped out of that tree and landed on your head?"

"Yes. It was, like, last night."

"My *point* is that you had no idea I was there."

"Well, I did, because I was there for you to land on."

"I'm a deadly weapon. Silent but deadly."

He barked out a laugh.

"What?"

"Silent but deadly. Pretty sure you just described a fart."

I rolled my eyes. "You're so mature."

"And you're silent but deadly. Like a fart."

"You know, I should have given this whole mate thing more thought."

With a playful growl, he swept me off my feet. I yelped and threw my arms around his neck. Damn his delicious strong arms and firm muscles. "You are absolutely incorrigible."

"And absolutely in love with you." He kissed me so thoroughly that for a moment I might have actually forgotten my own name. "Also, I love that you called it *our* palace."

"I love you too. Now let's get out of here." I smiled wide and kissed his cheek. "Portal us into *our* kitchen. I'm hungry."

"Of course you are." He pulled out an orb and dropped it into the middle of the hall. Our palace's large, sunny kitchen came into view on the other side, and my heart overflowed with joy as Grimm stepped over the threshold with me in his arms.

The sun shone bright through the large windows, enveloping us in light and warmth, while the scent of freshly baked pastries and pies tempted me almost as much as the wolf placing me on my feet. Off in the distance, the sound of music and laughter filled the air, most likely the staff enjoying their afternoon.

Grimm wrapped his arms around me, and I melted

against him. "It's good to be home," he said, brushing his lips over mine. "My fierce little ocelot prince."

I *was* fierce, fierce in my love for this amazing, at times infuriating, beautiful man, and I would spend the rest of my life showing him just how fiercely I loved him.

# EPILOGUE

## KING ALARICK

WHAT A DAY.

I unclasped my robe and tossed it on the bed before toeing off my shoes. When I walked over to the couch where Jean sat, he shifted to the end—because he knew me so well—and I flopped down to lie back and rest my head on his lap. My bedroom housed several exquisite furniture pieces, boasting the highest level of quality and comfort, yet nothing was as comfortable to me as Jean's lap. At the end of each day, my pleasure lay in putting my feet up with my head in his lap. He only had himself to blame for my being so spoiled, as he was the first to indulge my whims.

"I'm exhausted," I said with a sigh.

Jean chuckled. "You didn't do anything."

"Didn't I, though?"

"No, you didn't."

"I put the whole quest together!" I moaned in contentment when he put his hand on my head and stroked my hair. "I made phone calls and visited creepy forests, spoke to all those hounds."

"No. You said, 'I have a great idea,' proceeded to babble off nonsense I had to interpret and arrange into something actionable, to which you said 'yes, that!' Then *I* made phone calls, visited creepy forests, and spoke to all those hounds."

That didn't sound right. Did it? Sounded familiar, though. "I'm not sure you're recalling the events accurately."

"Oh, I recall very accurately."

I smiled up at him. "You're so good to me."

He hummed, and I ignored his amused smile. I wasn't wrong—but then I rarely ever was.

Jean was good to me. The best, really. I never understood why he chose to be my steward and advisor as his reward for saving my life all those thousands of years ago. He could have had anything—riches, power, magic. Instead, he chose to serve me, to be at my side. Over the years I'd attempted to give him various treasures, even a castle, but he'd just smile, thank me, and politely decline my offer, stating he already had everything he needed. Such an odd fellow. I supposed that's why we got on so well.

"Owin did so much better than I anticipated," I said, pleased. "Considering how stubborn he is, I worried his quest would take longer. Much, much, *much* longer. Still, I think that went rather well." Cat shifters were particularly feisty.

"Hmm, yes." Jean drummed his fingers on my brow. "Except for the part where Grimm almost killed the crocotta. You seem to be forgetting that little detail."

I cringed. "Yeah, that would have been bad. I hadn't expected him to be so... intense."

Jean went quiet for a heartbeat. "You never know what someone is capable of when it comes to protecting the one they love."

I leaned my head back to look up at him. "I suppose. Are you all right?"

"Of course. Why wouldn't I be?"

I shrugged. Jean was unflappable, an unbreakable force. Lately he seemed almost... distracted? No, not that, but something was certainly off. He'd never, in all the time I had known him, behaved in such a manner. I couldn't yet put my finger on it. I'd have said he was quiet, but then he was always reserved. He wasn't excitable or prone to bursts of outrage. "You'd tell me, wouldn't you? If something was troubling you?"

Jean smiled down at me, and I couldn't help but notice there was almost a sadness to that smile. "There's no one I trust more."

I frowned at his nonanswer. "Jean?"

"You keep frowning like that and you'll get wrinkles." He booped my nose, and I gasped, horrified.

"How can you say such a thing?"

He laughed, and I sat up, swiped a pillow off the couch, and batted him with it, which only made him laugh harder.

"You're terrible," I scolded, holding back my smile.

His laugh was wonderful, deep and gravelly. "Says the king attacking a blind man."

My jaw dropped. "You did not just say that to me." I whacked him again for good measure, and he threw his head back and laughed again. "So mean."

Jean shrugged, his smile impossibly wide. I moved in close to him and took his hand in mine, concerned by his sharp intake of breath.

"Jean? Are you sure you're okay? You're everything to

me. My truest friend. If there's something, anything that's bothering you, I want to help."

"Thank you." He patted my hand and stood. "Come. It's time to get you ready for bed, Your Majesty."

I noticed he did that often. Call me "Your Majesty" when he didn't want to continue a certain conversation. As if he were trying to put distance between us. All I could do was take him at his word. He was immortal, far too old for me to pester about sharing his feelings. He'd always been one to keep his emotions under strict control. I supposed one of us had to be the adult, as he liked to say.

"Fine. I do have a new quest to think about."

"You mean *I* have a new quest to think about," he said with a knowing smile.

"Funny."

Jean helped me out of my suit jacket and returned it to its hanger. I removed my pants and handed them to him, then sat on the bed to remove my socks as he hung up my suit.

"This next prince is going to be a challenge. He barely leaves his palace. Always hiding away in his library with his nose in a book."

Jean pursed his lips in thought as he approached. He held his hand out and took my socks from me. "I'm afraid we won't be able to send him on a merry chase the way we did with Owin. For all his feline snobbery, Owin was already adventurous. I worry too much nature will overwhelm the poor bear."

"He's a bear! He's supposed to love nature!" I slipped out of my shirt and handed it to Jean. "I'll never understand these young princes. In my day—"

"In your day dragons roamed the earth. No, wait, those were dinosaurs."

"I didn't realize you were a comedian as well as an advisor."

"I aim to please, my love."

I froze. "What?"

"What?" Jean asked.

"What did you say?"

"I said I aim to please, My Liege."

"Are you sure that's what you said?"

Jean frowned. "Yes. Why? What did you hear?"

I shook my head. "Nothing. I must be more tired than I thought. I think I'll have a bath."

"Are you sure?" Jean asked, following me to my royal en suite bathroom. "I don't want you falling asleep in the tub again."

"It's fine." I waved a hand in dismissal. It wasn't like I could drown or anything. Even asleep, my body reacted to any danger and shifted appropriately. "I'll just end up shifting into an otter or something."

"You mean like when you fell asleep in the pool and shifted into an alligator?"

I walked into the bathroom and stepped aside so he could get my bath ready. "It was humid that day. There's no humidity in here. Now, let's discuss the bear shifter prince." I was concerned for all the princes. Their quests would push them each to their limit, and beyond. "Do you think they'll be all right? What if I make the wrong choices and one of them *does* fail, Jean?"

Jean came to stand before me, his hands on my shoulders. "You must have faith in them, just as I have faith in you."

I covered his hands with mine and smiled. "Thank you, Jean. We'll get them through this. Together."

"Together."

UP NEXT

Continue the adventure with Prince Bernd and Saer's story in *The Prince and His Captivating Carpenter*, the second book in the Paranormal Princes series. Available on Amazon and KindleUnlimited.

# A NOTE FROM THE AUTHOR

THANK you so much for reading *The Prince and His Bedeviled Bodyguard*, the first book in the Paranormal Princes series. I hope you enjoyed Prince Owin and Grimm's adventures, and if you did, please consider leaving a review on Amazon. Reviews can have a significant impact on a book's visibility, so any support you show these fellas would be amazing. The adventure continues with Bernd and Saer's story in *The Prince and His Captivating Carpenter*, book two in the Paranormal Princes series, available from Amazon and KindleUnlimited.

A big thank you to Macy Blake for letting Prince Owin and Grimm visit her fabulous hellhounds. Want to read more about Solomon, Cody, or Walt? Check out Macy Blake's Hellhound Champions series on Amazon and KU!

Want to stay up-to-date on my releases and receive exclusive content? Sign up for my newsletter.

Follow me on Amazon to be notified of a new release, or

connect with me on social media, including my Facebook group, Donuts, Dog Tags, and Day Dreams, where we chat books, post pictures, have giveaways, and more!

Looking for inspirational photos of my books? Visit my book boards on Pinterest.

Thank you again for joining the fellas on their adventures. We hope to see you real soon!

Thick & Thin

Darkest Hour Before Dawn

Gummy Bears & Grenades

Tried & True

THIRDS Beyond the Books: Volume 1

THIRDS Beyond the Books: Volume 2

## THIRDS UNIVERSE TITLES

Love and Payne

## NORTH POLE CITY TALES

Mending Noel

The Heart of Frost

The Valor of Vixen

Loving Blitz

Disarming Donner

Courage and the King

North Pole City Tales Complete Series Paperback

## TITLES COMING SOON

## SOLDATI HEARTS

The Soldati Prince

The Foxling Soldati

## STANDALONE

Forgive and Forget

Finding Mr. Wrong

Beware of Geeks Bearing Gifts

Healing Hunter's Heart

Love in Retrograde

## AUDIOBOOKS

Check out the audio versions on Audible here.

## ABOUT THE AUTHOR

Charlie Cochet is the international bestselling author of the THIRDS series. Born in Cuba and raised in the US, Charlie enjoys the best of both worlds, from her daily Cuban latte to her passion for classic rock.

Currently residing in Central Florida, Charlie is at the beck and call of a rascally Doxiepoo bent on world domination. When she isn't writing, she can usually be found devouring a book, releasing her creativity through art, or binge watching a new TV series. She runs on coffee, thrives on music, and loves to hear from readers.

www.charliecochet.com

Sign up for Charlie's newsletter:
https://newsletter.charliecochet.com